The Sky Blue Frame

Frank took off his sweater and tossed it on a chair. He sat on his bed, testing the mattress. "Hey, look!" He picked up a small box that he found on his pillow. "A box of chocolates. Classy!" He lay down on the bed and began to untie the gold cord around the box. "This may be an old inn, but they do have some modern ideas."

He tugged at the top but pulled unevenly, and only one side came up. The box tilted, and all the dark chocolates spilled onto his shirt. He started to replace them one at a time. Just as he was reaching for the last piece—it moved.

A spider!

The Hardy Boys Mystery Stories

Available from MINSTREL Books

THE HARDY BOYS® MYSTERY STORIES

89

The
HARDY BOYS®

THE SKY
BLUE FRAME

FRANKLIN W. DIXON

A MINSTREL® BOOK

PUBLISHED BY POCKET BOOKS

New York   London   Toronto   Sydney   Tokyo   Singapore

This novel is a work of fiction. Names, characters, places and
incidents are either the product of the author's imagination or
are used fictitiously. Any resemblance to actual events or
locales or persons, living or dead, is entirely coincidental.

A MINSTREL PAPERBACK ORIGINAL

A Minstrel Book published by
POCKET BOOKS, a division of Simon & Schuster Inc.,
1230 Avenue of the Americas, New York, N Y 10020

Copyright © 1988 by Simon & Schuster Inc.
Cover artwork copyright © 1988 by Paul Bachem

Produced by Mega-Books of New York, Inc.

ISBN: 0-671-64974-4

First Minstrel Books printing March 1988

10 9 8 7 6 5 4

THE HARDY BOYS MYSTERY STORIES, A MINSTREL BOOK
and colophon are trademarks of Simon & Schuster Inc.

THE HARDY BOYS is a registered trademark
of Simon & Schuster Inc.

Printed in the U.S.A.

Contents

1 Caught in the Act

"He's disappeared!" Joe Hardy looked over his shoulder in annoyance.

"Who has?" Frank Hardy asked his younger brother, Joe. They were at the Bayport Mall, moving along with the steady stream of late-morning shoppers.

"Chet has! Where do you think he's gone?"

Frank scanned the immediate area. Then he pointed. "He's over there, beside the up escalator."

"That figures," said Joe, his eyes following the escalator up to the restaurants on the second level.

Frank grinned. "The only shopping he cares about is what he can find at the fast-food stands."

1

Chet, tall and heavyset, waved when he saw them approaching. "Hey, guys!" he called. "What do you say we check out the second floor? My stomach tells me it's just about lunchtime."

"According to your stomach, it's always time for lunch—or dinner or breakfast or dessert," Joe shot back good-naturedly. "But you're right, I am hungry. Let's see what's doing upstairs."

The Hardys looked around them as they stepped off the escalator. There were restaurants of all kinds—Chinese, Italian, Indian, Mexican, Japanese, even Hawaiian—and all of them smelled delicious. Chet rubbed his hands together. "I think I'll try—everything."

Joe looked at his brother. "I suddenly feel like pizza!"

"So do I!" agreed Frank, and they both headed for the Italian stand. Two slices of pizza and two lemonades later, they found Chet eating at one of the tables in the center dining section.

"How'd you get a table?" groaned Joe. "We had to eat standing up!"

Chet smiled knowingly. "I know my way around this place." He pushed the last of an egg roll into his mouth. "Okay, where to? I'm all yours now."

Suddenly, there was a commotion in the

2

crowd. Frank grabbed Joe's arm. "Did you see that?"

"What?" Joe asked, startled.

"That kid in the green sweater! He just snatched that woman's purse!" Frank tossed the words over his shoulder as he took off after the thief. Joe and Chet quickly joined in the pursuit.

The thief heard the boys' pounding feet behind him, because he bolted through a startled knot of shoppers, elbowing people out of the way. Everyone was too stunned to try to stop him.

The three teenagers barreled their way through the crowd—tamales, egg rolls, and chili dogs flying in all directions.

The thief raced to the wrong escalator and had to run down against the moving stairs, which slowed his escape. "Coming through!" he shouted as he pushed by the shoppers. Joe and Chet struggled behind him as Frank sped to the down escalator.

The purse snatcher was already on the ground floor and running at full speed by the time the boys made it down. "There he is," Joe yelled to Chet.

"Stop him!" Frank yelled. But people didn't know who to help, and instead stepped back from the chase, making a clear path for the thief.

The green sweater was clearly visible in the crowd as he darted toward the center of the mall near a large fountain.

"He's circling the fountain," cried Frank, signaling to the other two. "Head him off. I'll stay on his tail!"

Joe and Chet doubled back to the other side of the fountain, while shoppers watched openmouthed.

The thief rounded the fountain and looked back to see if his pursuers were still behind him. He paused, faked a move to the left, and then turned toward the nearest exit—only to find his path blocked by Chet, who stood like a husky, middle linebacker waiting for the ball carrier to come his way.

The thief easily sidestepped Chet and had a clear run to the exit. But in the next second he found himself sprawled out over the floor. Joe Hardy, hidden behind Chet's large hulk, had made good use of his long legs and tripped the escaping purse snatcher.

"Good work, Joe!" Frank said as he pulled the thief off the floor. He reached underneath the boy's green sweater. "This yours?" Frank asked, holding up the stolen purse. "I don't think red really goes with your outfit."

The captured thief beamed at the Hardys in admiration. "Hey, you guys are all right!" he said, grinning.

"Glad you like our work," Frank replied dryly. He raised his shoulders and shot Joe a questioning look.

"No kidding!" the thief continued. "It was great the way you split up and did an end run to head me off. Actually, I thought you'd catch me before I got to the escalator."

"I almost did," Frank answered. "But there were people in the way—wait a minute! You sound like you're *glad* we caught you!"

"Yeah, what is this?" Joe asked.

"I think I can explain." An enormous man in a light gray suit picked his way through the crowd that had gathered around the boys.

Frank, Joe, and Chet turned to face the balding, fat man. Directly behind him was the elderly woman whose purse had been snatched. The two of them were smiling broadly.

"Who are you?" Joe and Frank asked, giving the man a once-over.

The man laughed. "Well, what do you say, Maggie? Do you think this has gone far enough? Here's your purse back." He took the purse and handed it over to the woman. "I'm sure everything's there." He gave the boy in the green sweater a playful pat on the shoulder. "Good work, Jim!"

Then he turned to the crowd around them. "It's okay, folks. Everything's fine." The shoppers began to disperse slowly.

Frank and Joe looked at each other in total confusion.

"Would you please let us in on all the fun?" Frank asked, very irritated.

"Yeah, what is this? Some kind of hidden-camera TV show?" Chet asked, looking around for equipment.

The man smiled. "No, I'm afraid it's not. But it was planned. Let's sit down and talk."

"Planned?" Frank repeated, taking a seat opposite the man. This was getting weirder and weirder. He wanted an explanation—now.

The heavy man produced a card from his wallet. "Allow me to introduce myself. My name is Mark R. Maxwell." He placed his hand on the woman's shoulder and said, "This is my friend Maggie Sills, and her grandson, Jim. I arranged this scene with them for your benefit."

"You mean the whole thing was faked?" Joe asked. He felt anger rising inside him.

Frank was having difficulty hiding his annoyance. "For our *benefit*? What are you talking about?"

"It's all very simple," explained Mr. Maxwell. "I was testing you. I wanted to see if you're as good as I've heard you are. And I must admit, you do your reputations justice."

"You've heard of us?" Joe asked.

"Anyone who reads the newspapers has heard of the Hardy boys. Come now, don't be so modest. You are Fenton Hardy's sons, aren't you?"

"Yes, that's right," Frank said.

A gleam appeared in Maxwell's eyes. "We followed you into the mall and set up this little incident so we could see you in action."

Maggie and her grandson smiled a bit sheepishly. "We really had you fooled, didn't we?" Maggie said with a giggle.

"You certainly did." Frank forced a smile. Then he gave Maxwell a hard look. "Okay, we appreciate your little joke, but there's one question you haven't answered. *Why?*"

Maxwell chuckled. But when he realized he was laughing by himself, he abruptly stopped and turned serious. "All right, let's get down to business! I like the way you boys handle yourselves. Frankly, I'm impressed!" He paused.

"We appreciate the compliment," said Frank.

Maxwell took a cigar out of his coat pocket and rolled it carefully between his fingers. "I have a business proposition for you."

Joe moved forward, his blue eyes steely. "Okay," he said, still wary. "As long as it's on the up-and-up."

Maxwell looked down at the floor for a moment as if in deep thought. Finally, he looked up first at Joe, then into Frank's dark brown eyes. "Well, it isn't, *exactly*. You see, I want you two to commit a crime!"

2 The Crime of the Century

"Mister, you've made a big mistake!" Frank stood up and stared down at Maxwell. "We're not criminals!" he said harshly.

"Right!" Joe agreed. He and Frank turned to leave with Chet.

They stopped and turned back when Maxwell began to laugh. He was laughing so hard, he had to take out his handkerchief and dab at his eyes.

"Sorry, I'm afraid I didn't phrase that quite right," he said between gasps. "I don't want you to commit a *real* crime! Nothing could be further from the truth!"

Maxwell put his handkerchief away. "Look at the card I just gave you. As you can see, I own the

Sky Blue Inn in the mountains. Have you ever heard of mystery weekends?"

Frank was the first to answer. "Sure. Guests are invited to spend the weekend at a hotel or lodge. There's a fake mystery—a murder, robbery, or a kidnapping. Then the guests try to solve the crime before the weekend's over."

"Exactly," said Mr. Maxwell.

"So what's that got to do with us?" Joe asked.

"A lot," Maxwell replied smugly. "You two have solved a few mysteries in your day, am I right?"

Frank and Joe looked slightly embarrassed. "Let's just say we helped whenever we could," Frank said.

Maxwell chewed on his unlit cigar for a moment. "Well, what I want you to do is come up with a mystery for our guests to solve. Execute the crime, leave clues, cast suspicion on various guests—in other words, stage the whole thing!"

Frank and Joe grinned. They loved the idea.

Maxwell continued. "I can't pay much, but you and a couple of friends will get a free weekend in the mountains!"

Now both Hardys were really interested. "You mean we can invite our friends?" They looked at Chet, who was grinning broadly.

Maxwell laughed. "Of course. I expect you'll need accomplices for your—ah, crime."

"We could invite Chet and Iola," Frank suggested. "And Callie! How many friends can we bring?"

"Better limit it to two or three," Maxwell cautioned. "After all, we'll need rooms for our paying guests."

"Sounds great!" Joe said.

Maxwell held up his hand. "There's something I haven't told you," he said. Then he paused, rolling his cigar between his fingers as he chose his words. The boys waited for him to continue.

"Planning a fake mystery is not the only reason I've invited you to the inn. There have been a series of hotel robberies in the area, and I thought you might be able to snoop around a little. The police are baffled so far, and you might be able to come up with something they've missed."

Joe, his blue eyes flashing in anticipation, slapped his brother on the back. "How about that? We get to plan a fake crime for the entertainment of the guests, and work on a *real* mystery too!"

"I gather that means you'll do it," Maxwell said as he reached in his pocket for a match.

"Wait a minute," said Frank. "What weekend are we talking about?"

"In three weeks," Maxwell replied. "That'll give you boys time to plan, and give me a chance to advertise. I've run some teaser ads. You know, one of those 'Do you love a good mystery? Watch this space for information on the caper of your life at the Sky Blue Inn.' I think we've whetted enough appetites by now, so when I put the real ad in, we should have no trouble attracting guests."

Maxwell finally lit his cigar. He took a couple of puffs and blew a heavy cloud of brown smoke into the air. "Then it's settled," he said, and removed a long white envelope from an inner pocket in his jacket.

"Here are some general instructions and directions to the inn. You shouldn't have any trouble finding it."

Frank accepted the envelope. Then both Hardys shook hands with Maxwell to seal the deal. "Oh, just one more thing. When you've roughed out your plans, drop a copy in the mail to me. Not at the inn. Use the P.O. box on my card. I don't want anyone else to know."

"Sure. We'll keep you posted," agreed Frank. He gave Maxwell the thumbs-up sign.

Maxwell waved his cigar at them and said, "See you two weeks from Friday!" He headed toward a nearby exit with Maggie and her grandson, cigar smoke following in their wake. Frank and Joe slapped each other a high-five.

With Maxwell out of earshot, Chet said, "That cigar smelled like he was smoking old socks!"

"It did clean out my sinuses," agreed Joe. "Let's move out!"

Frank started toward the north corridor. "I want to check out the sporting goods store at the other end of the mall," he said.

Chet edged away in the opposite direction and tugged on Joe's arm. "How about another little side trip up the escalator?" he inquired, lifting his eyebrows comically.

"No way . . ." Joe started to say as he turned to nudge Chet back. But his attention was drawn to a figure that seemed to be staring at him from the up escalator. It was a biker in black leather. A huge snake decal twisted its way around the black motorcycle helmet he wore. And the full visor was flipped down to cover his face. It made him look like a twentieth-century Darth Vader.

The biker raised his hand in what Joe thought would be a greeting. But the hand stopped short just beneath the helmet. Then the biker slowly drew his index finger across his throat! Reaching the top of the escalator, he quickly stepped off and melted into the crowd above.

That evening the three boys were in the Hardys' kitchen making plans.

Joe spread out Maxwell's instructions and literature on the kitchen table. "I checked with Dad. He said he'd be glad to help out if we want."

"Look at this." Joe held up a brochure describing the Sky Blue Inn. "They've got a swimming pool, a tennis court—"

"It's too cold to go swimming this time of year," Frank interrupted. "But if we have time, we might sneak in a little tennis."

"I doubt it. Maxwell was serious about those hotel robberies," Joe said.

"You're right. Check these out." Frank tossed him several newspaper clippings about the rash of burglaries that summer.

"Looks like the work of the same person," Joe said thoughtfully when he finished reading.

"Or persons," said Frank, correcting him. "Did you notice? All of the robberies have taken place within the past month."

"So whoever's responsible is new to the area," Joe commented.

"Maybe, maybe not," Frank said. "But we

14

can't do anything about those robberies until we get up there."

Joe nodded. "Enough about real crimes. Let's get down to business and plan our own mystery!"

Chet turned his chair around and straddled it. "Yeah, let's really fake 'em out," he said eagerly.

"Iola's definitely coming, right?" Joe asked hopefully. He and Chet's sister had been going out for some time.

"Yep," confirmed Chet. "Says she wouldn't miss it. Too bad Callie can't go, though."

Frank grimaced. "She's going away to visit her grandparents that weekend. But I've got a great idea on how we can use Iola."

"How?" asked Chet.

"I'm going to make her the 'victim' of the crime. Does Iola have anything that looks expensive but really isn't? You know, like some kind of fancy-looking jewelry?"

Chet thought for a moment. "I hardly ever notice what my sister wears. Wait a minute! She does have a rhinestone necklace that looks like real diamonds, at least that's what everyone says."

"Sounds perfect!" said Frank. "But I'd like to see it first."

"Iola's home now. Should we go check it out?" Chet asked.

Frank's dark head and Joe's blond one nodded at the same time. "After we finish up here," said Frank.

"So, who's going to be the thief?" Chet asked, after an hour of planning.

Frank looked up at him, grinning slyly. "You are, old buddy."

Chet was so astonished he couldn't speak for a moment. "Me?" he finally choked out.

"Right!" Frank said. "And we'll pretend that Iola is our sister and that none of us know you."

"But me, a thief?" Chet asked as they threw on their coats, ready to go see Iola's necklace. "Why me?"

Frank and Joe laughed. "Because of that angel face," Joe said. "Who could ever suspect a face like this?" He pinched Chet's chubby cheeks.

"I'm getting out of here," said Chet.

On the sidewalk the boys looked up at the half-moon, a feathery wisp of clouds drifting gently across its face. With their attention on the night sky, they didn't notice the large black limousine that had turned the corner and was driving toward them.

They did notice the car, though—and fast—when it picked up speed and came barreling down the road at them. An electric window lowered steadily, and the boys caught sight of a gloved hand as it flashed out and then withdrew into the darkness of the car.

"Duck!" Joe shouted as he hurled himself to the ground to avoid the brick coming straight at him!

3 Uneasy Riders

After picking himself up, Frank reached for the brick. Attached to it with a rubber band was a note on plain white paper. He read the note aloud.

"If you know what's good for you—
you'll stay away from the Sky Blue Inn.
P.S. We've got Iola Morton!"

"Let's go back inside and call your house to see if Iola really is gone," Frank said to Chet, who had gone white as a sheet. Joe had already darted into the house.

Joe had just finished punching the numbers

18

into the wall phone beside the refrigerator and was waiting for it to ring when Chet and Frank came through the kitchen door.

"Hi, Mrs. Morton, this is Joe. Is Iola there? . . . She went out? . . . Did she say when she'd be back? . . . Oh, nothing. Just tell her I called. . . . Yeah, Chet is still here. Okay. 'Bye." Joe hung up, his eyes filled with worry and fear.

"Okay, now what do we do?" Chet asked, his voice shaking.

"Usually we wait for a second message. But this note gives us no instructions. I wonder if it's a phony."

Joe shook his head. "I've got a feeling on this one, Frank," he said. "She's gone. And I'm not just going to wait around. You guys stay here by the phone, but I'm going to look for her."

"Hey, she's my sister," Chet said. "I'm going, too. I'd be useless here, anyway."

Frank agreed to stay by the phone, and the other two headed for the van. Halfway there Joe realized he had misplaced his keys and sprinted back for Frank's.

"Can I have your keys?" he asked, slightly out of breath.

"Are you okay? You're not too upset to drive?" Frank asked with concern.

"No, I'm fine. Or I will be as soon as we get Iola back. What do you really think? Is that note real or phony?"

"I can't call it. But it's funny there were no instructions. Joe, be careful. We have no idea who we're dealing with."

Joe tore around the side of the house and back to the front curb. Chet was waiting next to the van, shivering slightly in his T-shirt. "Why didn't you get in?" Joe asked.

"Can't. It's locked."

"Locked? That's weird. We never lock it in front of the house. Well, come on. Climb in," said Joe, unlocking the door.

"Where do we start?" asked Chet.

"Your mom said that Iola had gone over to Callie's, so that's where we're going first," Joe answered, turning the key in the ignition. "Wait a minute, did you hear something?"

"Only the engine. Wait—I do hear something. It sounds like, like pounding."

Joe climbed over the rear seat. And there, with her hands and feet bound together, was Iola! She had a piece of white adhesive tape over her mouth.

"Iola, are you all right?" Joe asked as he gently peeled the tape off her mouth.

20

"I will be as soon as I get my hands on those bozos. They said they wouldn't hurt me and that you'd find me right away. They also told me to tell you that this is a warning. They want you to know how easily they can get to you. And they want you to stay away from the Sky Blue Inn."

Joe and Chet helped Iola out of the van and, each holding an arm, walked her into the house.

"Hail the conquering warriors," Chet said to Frank as he entered the kitchen.

"You've got her already?"

"They tied her up and put her in the back of your van."

"Iola," Frank said, "are you okay?"

"I will be as soon as I get to tape and truss a couple of turkeys myself."

"Are we sure we want to go through with this mystery weekend? It's beginning to look like more than we bargained for," Chet said with a worried frown.

"Well, if someone thinks a threat is going to stop me from checking out a mystery, he's very wrong," Joe said emphatically. "But maybe you should stay home, Iola. I couldn't stand it if anything happened to you."

"No! I'm with you all the way. I want to find whoever did this to me! Hand me your plans,

Frank. Maybe I can come up with some brilliant ideas of my own for our mystery weekend."

Frank and Joe smiled and slid the papers across the table to Iola.

"The inn's fairly small—it only has room for about a dozen guests," Joe said, filling her in. "Which makes it perfect for this kind of weekend. Things could get out of hand if we had to deal with a lot of guests."

A flicker of excitement gleamed in Iola's green eyes as she read. "It'll be like going back in time. There aren't any televisions or radios in the rooms. Just one TV set in the lobby."

"Oh, no! You mean no TV or music!" Chet groaned. "I don't know if I can make it!"

"Relax, Chet," Frank said, "we're going to be too busy to notice the lack of entertainment."

Joe chuckled. "After all, you've got a robbery to pull off!"

Chet moaned. "Oh, brother! I forgot about that!"

The next three weeks passed without further incident. They checked out Iola's necklace and firmed up their plans. Before they knew it, the Hardys were packing the van for their mystery weekend.

Coming out of the house with the tennis racket he'd almost left behind, Frank was pleasantly surprised to see Callie Shaw leaning against the van.

"I couldn't let you leave without saying good-bye," she said, smiling.

Frank put his tennis racket in the back next to his bag. "I'm glad you came."

"I wish I could go with you, but you know my parents. This trip to my grandma's was planned weeks ago."

"Well, think of all the interesting things we'll have to talk about when I get back." He grinned at her and gave her arm a reassuring squeeze.

Chet, Iola, and Joe came dashing from the house. "All set?" Frank asked.

They nodded.

"Then let's hit the road," said Joe. He jumped into the front seat, while Frank slid behind the wheel and Chet and Iola piled into the back. Frank leaned out the window and said to Callie, "See you Monday!"

"Have a safe trip," she called back. "And a good mystery!"

"We're going to baffle them," Joe shouted as the van disappeared around the corner.

* * *

23

Bayport soon faded behind them, and Frank left the local roads to nose the car onto the highway. The drive to the mountains would take about three hours, which would put them at the Sky Blue Inn around two o'clock.

"That'll give us plenty of time to check ourselves in and then check out all the guests," said Frank.

Iola giggled. "I'll be sure to wear my *diamond* necklace down for dinner!"

Chet snorted. "Don't you wish!"

"But it looks real!" Iola said. "You all said it did. It would take an expert to tell the difference!"

"That's what you said about that gold ring you bought," Chet said. "Until your finger turned green!"

"I hope we're right, Iola," Frank said. "Your necklace is going to be put to the test in just a few hours!"

The morning traffic was light, and Frank kept to a steady fifty-five miles per hour. Joe was content watching the scenery, while Chet and Iola dozed in the backseat.

They drove quietly that way for over an hour. Growing tired of the scenery, Joe glanced over at Frank. His brother's face was tense.

"What's up?" Joe asked, instantly alert.

"You look like you have something on your mind."

Frank's eyes had been on the road, but now they flicked up to the rearview mirror. "Look behind us."

Joe turned, pretending to be engaged in conversation with his friends in the backseat. "What? All I see is a motorcycle, Frank. What's up?"

"That bike has been behind us for the past hour. He's just closed the gap. And check out that cycle!"

Frank slowed down so Joe could take a closer look. The cycle was entirely black, except for a decal of a coiled yellow snake on its front fender. The rider was also in black, with a matching decal on his helmet!

"Uh-oh," said Joe. "You thinking what I'm thinking?"

"I don't know," Frank admitted. "It may just be a coincidence, but it's pretty weird that he's dressed just like that guy in the mall. Maybe they're members of the same gang. I'll slow down even more and see if he passes."

Frank dropped the van's speed down. "I'm at forty-five now. Let's see how he likes that."

The motorcycle slowed and continued to follow them.

"Slow down some more," Joe suggested, still watching through the rear window.

Frank lifted his foot from the accelerator until the speedometer read only forty miles an hour.

"I shouldn't go any slower on this road," he said.

The biker reduced his speed to match theirs.

"Hang on. We're going to try it the other way," Frank said as his foot hit the accelerator. The speedometer rose steadily—forty-five, fifty, fifty-five.

The motorcycle kept pace with them.

"I don't get it," Chet said sleepily. He'd been listening to the goings-on with half-closed eyes.

"Neither do I," said Frank. They drove along in silence for a few minutes, all the time keeping tabs on the rider behind them.

Tension mounted in the van. Only the sounds of its tires spinning along the empty road and the steady hum of the motorcycle behind them could be heard.

Finally Frank said, "I've had enough of this!"

Frank pressed his foot down on the accelerator, and the speedometer jumped to sixty-five.

An ugly roar from the motorcycle told them that the biker had no intention of losing them.

"Want to play games, eh?" Frank muttered under his breath as he pushed the van to maintain its high speed on the hills they were beginning to climb.

"Frank, what do you think this is, the Grand Prix?" cried Iola, waking up as they flew around a curve.

"Okay, buddy. Follow me," said Frank. He yanked the wheel hard to the right and tore across two lanes to spin off onto an exit ramp.

The motorcycle was caught off guard and barely made the turn. Its tires whined in protest. Leaning far to the right, the biker almost hit the pavement. But he righted the bike at the last possible second and followed them onto the ramp.

"Almost lost him that time," cried Joe.

"For good," said Frank as he raced to the toll booth. "Okay, what do we do?"

"Don't slow down! Just go through! We'll send them the money later," shouted Joe.

With a loud alarm screaming, Frank zipped past a startled toll collector. He glanced in the rearview mirror to check on the bike. The rider roared past without paying, too.

Frank drove hard down the lonely backcountry road, pushing the van to its limit on straightaways and taking curves in the middle of the road, never braking, only lifting his foot from the accelerator to decrease his speed.

"He's gaining on us," yelled Chet, who was keeping a constant vigil out the back window with Iola.

"That's okay," muttered Frank. "I've got a few more tricks of my own"

A hill rose before them. And as the van crested it, Frank realized that on the other side, for seconds only, they would be out of the biker's sight. A grassy road branched off to his right. Frank spun the car onto it and drove a hundred feet into a thick stand of trees.

Turning in their seats, they saw the motorcycle speed by. Waiting just a moment, Frank gunned his engine, flipped the van into reverse, and doubled back the way they had just come.

"He bought it!" cried Chet. "He thinks we're still ahead of him! As long as we're off the main highway, why don't we stop for lunch?"

"No way," replied Frank. "I want to put a lot of distance between us and that guy."

They drove on for several miles, until they saw a billboard for a hamburger place. The brightly colored red and yellow sign told them that they were approachng Mr. Burger, with the slogan "Just Good Food" written under it.

"I don't know about you guys, but I'm starved," Iola said. "Let's see if Mr. Burger knows what he's talking about."

"Anything would be fine with me at this point," said Chet, his face up against the window.

Frank turned and drove a mile down another road to Mr. Burger. After a hearty lunch of burgers, shakes, and fries, they left the restaurant with renewed energy. "Mr. Burger is a man of his word," Chet said, running his tongue over his lips. "Those burgers were . . ."

Chet never completed his sentence. Joe and Frank were already sprinting to the far end of the parking lot, where a motorcycle was turning onto the road. A black motorcycle, with a yellow snake on its fender.

"Come on," Frank shouted, "let's follow him in the car!"

The Hardys ran back to the van, but they stopped dead in their tracks when they saw Chet and Iola's expressions.

"Guess what, guys?" Iola said. "We're not going anywhere." She pointed to the right front fender. Joe and Frank looked. The tire had been slashed!

4 Checking In — Checking Out

The tire was ruined. "Oh, no," Frank groaned. "And no spare. Joe blew *that* last week. We'll have to call a garage."

"I wonder why the biker slashed only one tire," Joe said. "Why not all four?"

"We probably interrupted him," said Iola.

"I'm not so sure about that," Frank said doubtfully.

A quick phone call to a nearby garage brought a truck with a new tire. Forty-five minutes later they were on the highway again. "We're not too far behind schedule," Frank said. "Even with all our problems!"

After an hour of driving, Frank said, "We're

30

getting close. Keep your eyes open for signs for the inn."

No sooner had he spoken than a bright bill-board advertising the inn loomed up at the side of the road. As they passed it, Chet and Joe turned, hearing an engine rev up.

Behind the sign was a black motorcycle. Its driver straddled the bike, motionless. He revved up the engine one last time but remained where he was, watching the van as it disappeared around a curve.

Less than five minutes later Frank turned the car onto the exit ramp. They rode in silence, craning their necks, looking for the inn. Sudden-ly they all exclaimed together, "There it is!"

Frank stopped the car. As planned, they let Chet off at the gate so he could arrive after them. Then they drove through the stone pillars that marked the entrance and up a long gravel drive-way lined with trees. It wound back and forth up a hill. Finally, it opened out at the inn, a ram-bling, old Victorian house with several peaked gables on the roof.

A large green lawn rolled out for several hun-dred feet on either side until it disappeared into the surrounding woods. "Looks like it could be haunted," Iola said, shuddering.

Frank parked the van in the lot provided for guests. They removed their baggage and hurried up the steps to the front door.

Once inside, they found themselves in an oak-paneled hallway dominated by a dark oak staircase that curved to the left as it rose to the second floor. Standing below, they could see it spiral upward all the way to the third floor. The hallway stretched straight back to the rear of the inn.

To their right, what once had been a small sitting room was now a lobby. To their left was a parlor, where two couples, both in their thirties, were seated.

"I think we check in here," said Frank, motioning toward the lobby. The threesome picked up their bags and moved forward to the desk.

A comfortable old leather couch occupied most of one wall of the lobby. Opposite it were a couple of armchairs separated by a table with a reading lamp on it. At the far side of the room was a counter where the desk clerk sat. Behind him was a small office with a large desk and a wall of pigeonholes that held the room keys.

The desk clerk was so engrossed in his newspaper that he failed to notice Iola and the Hardys approach. When Frank cleared his throat and said, "Hi," the desk clerk leapt to his feet with a start and dropped his paper.

"Excuse me, I didn't hear you enter," he said nervously. He was a small, thin man with a balding head over which he had carefully arranged a few strands of dark hair. His eyes darted around constantly.

Frank made the introductions. "I'm Frank Hardy, and this is my brother, Joe—"

Iola interrupted. "And I'm their sister!"

The desk clerk nodded his head and attempted to smile. "I'm Fred Peevey. Welcome to the Sky Blue Inn." As he spoke, he absently began to spin a silver dollar on the counter with his left hand. With his right, he leafed through a ledger until he came to the correct date. "Ah! Here you are. You have reservations for two rooms. Sign the register, and I'll get your keys."

While they signed in, Peevey got their keys from the office. He handed one to Frank and the other to Iola. "You fellows will be sharing room 207. Your sister will be right across the hall in room 206. Is that satisfactory?"

"Perfect." Frank smiled.

"I assumed you'd want to be close to each other," said Mr. Peevey, trying to be hospitable.

Joe was taking in the lobby. "This certainly is nice."

Peevey smiled. "Mr. Maxwell, the current owner, had it restored a few years ago. We've worked hard to retain its original flavor."

"He certainly did a terrific job. Where is Mr. Maxwell, anyway?" Frank asked.

Mr. Peevey said, "Oh, he's not here. He's away on business."

The Hardys couldn't conceal their surprise. "Away on business?" Frank asked. "I assumed he'd be here."

"Do you know him?" Peevey asked with interest.

At once Frank realized his mistake. He wasn't sure if Peevey was in on their secret.

Frank coughed. "No, not really. I just thought that the owner would be here, that's all."

"I see," replied Peevey. "Mr. Maxwell is away somewhere, looking for more antiques, I believe."

Joe decided to change the subject. "This is a great place, Mr. Peevey. I feel like we've been in a time machine and were sent back a hundred years!"

"Yes, the inn does have that feeling, doesn't it?" he said, warming to the subject. "Sometimes at night, I sit here and imagine what it was like back then."

"Do you have horseback riding here?" Joe asked.

"No," Peevey answered sadly. "The stable isn't used anymore. However, we do have a graveyard in back!"

"A g-graveyard?" Iola stammered. "You mean there's a graveyard right here on the grounds of this inn, and I'm going to be spending the night here?"

Peevey's smile was slightly sinister. "That's the way it used to be. Families would bury their loved ones on their own property."

"That gives me the creeps." Iola shuddered.

Peevey grinned, showing his yellow teeth. "But surely you're not afraid of graveyards?"

Frank didn't smile. "No, we're not."

Iola looked at the two Hardys and said, "All the same, I'm glad you two are just across the hall from me!"

Peevey lifted the countertop so he could join them in the lobby. "Let me show you around before I take you to your rooms. You must meet some of the other guests."

They followed him across the hall into the parlor where there were now six people conversing. "Excuse me, everyone," Peevey said. "We have three more guests for the weekend. This is Iola and Frank and Joe Hardy." The bell on the counter at the front desk sounded. Peevey excused himself and went back into the lobby.

An attractive girl in her early twenties rose to greet the "Hardys." She extended her hand. "Hi, I'm Julie Spaulding. Nice to meet you."

They shook hands and she turned to introduce them to the others. "This is Matt Spyle."

Matt, who was short and skinny, looked at them through horn-rimmed glasses. He was about the same age as Julie. "Hi, did you come up for the mystery weekend?" he asked, sitting down again.

"We did," admitted Joe. "Do you know anything about it?" He tried to look as innocent as possible.

"Only what I read in the newspaper ad. But I love a good mystery," Matt said excitedly, rubbing the palms of his hands on his knees. "I'm always reading them. Are you into mysteries, too?" He spoke so quickly that the others had to turn and focus on him to catch all his words.

Joe nodded his head and glanced at his brother. "All the time." He grinned at Matt.

Iola and the boys then met the two older

couples—the Faheys and Martins. They had already struck up a friendship, and the Hardys knew they would probably spend all their time together.

After they were seated, Julie asked, "Just when is this mystery weekend supposed to begin? I checked in around noon, and so far, nothing's happened!"

Joe shrugged. "The way we understand it is that at some point during the weekend, a crime will be committed. Then, it'll be up to the guests to figure out 'who done it.'"

"I wish something would happen soon," Julie complained. "I'm getting fidgety."

Just then a tall, muscular, blond young man strutted into the room. From his manner it was obvious that he thought a lot of himself. "Well, well," he began, "who have we here?" He was eyeing the entire group.

Frank decided he had to be the first to meet anyone that obnoxious. He extended his hand. "I'm Frank Hardy. Pleased to meet you."

The blond youth looked at Frank's hand for a moment as if it were a snake. Finally, he reached out to shake it and said, "I'm Brad. Brad Wilcox. I suppose you came up for this so-called mystery weekend, too."

"Well, why are you here?" Joe asked.

"I wanted to see if playing detective is all that it's cracked up to be," Brad admitted grudgingly.

"Meaning what?" asked Frank.

"Meaning I don't think detectives are anything special. Any idiot can solve a crime."

"And you want to prove that you're an idiot?" Joe asked.

Matt laughed raucously until a look from Brad shut him up. Matt then ran his hands over his knees, stood up quickly, and excused himself.

Brad simply smirked at Joe. "We'll see how smart we are this weekend!" Then he turned on his heel and followed Matt out of the room.

Julie whispered to Iola. "Isn't he gorgeous!"

"Oh, yes," Iola agreed. "A gorgeous jerk!"

After they'd talked for a while longer, Iola said, "Where's Mr. Peevey? I'd like to get up to my room and unpack."

Mr. Peevey magically appeared in the doorway. "This way," he said, and called out, "Mr. Botts! Mr. Botts!"

A huge, muscle-bound man, with black hair cut so short his scalp showed through, appeared next to Peevey. "Botts is our handyman, security guard, and jack-of-all-trades," explained Peevey. "Botts, would you take the Hardys' bags upstairs, please?"

"Yes, Mr. Peevey." Botts lifted their bags in his ham fists so easily that anyone would've thought they were empty. "This way."

As Frank, Joe, and Iola followed Botts up the stairs, they heard a commotion. Glancing down, they saw Mr. Peevey greeting Chet at the front door.

"I'm Chet Morton," he was saying. "I just came up on the bus."

"Right this way," they heard Peevey say. "Come sign the register, and I'll get your key."

Frank and Joe exchanged glances. Everything was going according to plan.

Once inside their room, the Hardys unpacked their bags and put away their clothes. Then Frank said, "I feel kind of grubby—I think I'll change."

He took off his sweater and tossed it on a chair. All the furniture in the room was Victorian. The two beds had heavy iron frames and stood high off the floor. He sat on his bed, testing the mattress.

"Soft, but the springs are firm," he said. "Hey, look here!" He picked up a small box that he found on his pillow. "A box of chocolates! Classy!"

Frank lay down on the bed and began to untie

the gold cord around the box of chocolates. He tugged at the top but pulled unevenly, and only one side came up. The box tilted, and all the dark chocolates spilled onto his shirt.

He started to replace them one at a time. Just as he was reaching for the last piece—it moved.

A spider!

5 Inn Trouble

Frank lay motionless. The grotesque, hairy creature raised itself on its eight legs and inched its way slowly up Frank's arm, moving toward his neck. Frank had no way of knowing if the spider was poisonous or not. But he couldn't take a chance—the slightest movement might cause it to bite!

There was nothing he could do except lie rigid and hope the spider crawled off him and onto the bed.

From the corner of his eye, Frank caught a glimpse of movement near his left side, then a flash of white. It was followed by a jet of rushing air and a loud snap!

Joe had flicked a towel across Frank, knocking

the spider onto the floor. He then rushed over to where it lay and tapped it lightly with a rolled-up magazine. He remained crouched there, examining the spider.

Frank sat up on the bed and took his first deep breath in two minutes. "That was too close! Someone deliberately put that spider in the candy box!" exclaimed Frank. "But who? And why?"

"Good questions," said Joe. He lifted the dead spider off the floor with a sheet of paper. "It's just an ordinary black spider. The whole scheme was meant to scare us, that's all."

Frank wiped his brow. "Well, it worked," he said, laughing a little shakily.

A look of concern crossed Joe's face as he studied his brother. "Still shook up?"

Frank's expression became grim. "No! Angry is more like it!" He squeezed his brother's shoulder. "And it's a good thing—because I have a feeling things are going to get a lot rougher before we're through!"

He shook his head in bewilderment. "What gets me is, we're just up here to stage a phony crime for the entertainment of the guests!"

"Don't you think this has something to do with the hotel robberies Mr. Maxwell told us about?" Joe asked his brother.

"You're right. It's the most logical explanation," replied Frank. "I guess the thieves don't want us snooping around."

"How do they know who we are?" Joe was puzzled. "Nobody really knows the reason we're here. I don't think even Peevey's been told."

Suddenly Joe tensed. "Oh, no!"

Frank stood up as Joe rushed toward the door. "What's the matter?"

"Iola!" Joe called over his shoulder. "They went after her once before!"

Frank rushed out the door behind Joe, who was already banging on Iola's door.

"Iola!" Joe cried.

The door opened slowly, and Iola peeked out at them curiously. "Something wrong? You guys look as though you've seen a ghost!" She pulled her heavy terry-cloth robe tighter around herself.

"Can we come in?" Joe asked.

"Well, I was just going to take a shower . . . but, okay."

Inside her room Frank told her about the spider, and she spoke her thoughts out loud. "This is even more serious than we guessed."

"We'd like to check out your room. Okay?" Frank asked.

"I've already done it, but go ahead if it'll make you feel better. I have to go in and turn off the shower." A blast of hot, heavy air drifted out of the bathroom and hit them like a wall before she shut the door behind her.

"She sure likes a hot shower," Frank said. They then turned to the matter of checking out her room, which took a few minutes and yielded nothing.

"It's taking her too long in there," said Joe, noticing Iola hadn't returned. "Iola, are you all right?" No answer. "Iola?" Again no answer. Both boys rushed to the door.

Locked! Why would Iola lock the door just to turn off the shower? "Iola, can you hear me?" When no answer came this time, Joe shoved against the door to force it open. The heavy oak door was swollen from the heat, and it took him three running tries to push it in.

They were blinded by the steam, and had difficulty breathing the water-heavy air. The steam was thickest around the shower and they had to grope through it to find the handle of the glass stall door. It gave after a couple of heavy tugs.

Frank grabbed a towel, wrapped it around his hand, and bent over to turn off the scalding hot water. Joe knelt down and picked up Iola's limp form.

Her thick terry-cloth robe weighed twenty

pounds from all the water it had soaked up. But it had saved her from a bad burn. Joe put her down gently on the bed.

Slowly she came to from her steambath and tried to sit up. But instantly she fell back again, her head wobbling. "Oh, am I dizzy," she groaned. "Someone must have been hiding behind the bathroom door, because after I opened the shower door, I felt a hand against my back. It shoved me, and the last thing I remember was hitting my head on the tile wall."

After they made sure Iola really was okay, the boys rushed back into the bathroom. They could see more clearly because the steam had started to evaporate. Directly opposite them was another door. Connecting rooms! That was how the intruder had gotten in and out. They knocked on the other door, but no one answered. They nudged it open and peered in. It had to be Julie's room, because they saw the clothes she had worn earlier on the bed. But Julie wasn't there.

Iola had gotten up by then and checked to make sure she wasn't burned. The heavy robe *had* protected her.

Frank and Joe tried to convince her to return home. But she stubbornly refused. After they realized their pleading was useless, they left her to finish dressing for dinner.

Out in the hall Frank glanced to the left and saw Botts. He was standing and staring at them as if mesmerized. Without a word of greeting, he turned and trudged away.

The Hardys decided to give their own room a good going-over. As they searched, Frank noticed something gleaming under his bed. Before touching it, he pulled out his pen flashlight and shone the beam on the gleaming object. "It looks like a coin," he said.

He carefully slid his hand under the bed, grasped the object, and brought it out.

"It's a silver dollar!" he said, rather amazed. "How did that get under—?"

The brothers looked at each other and mouthed the single word together. "Peevey!"

Frank sat on the floor, turning the coin over and over in his hand. "Our Mr. Peevey likes to spin a silver dollar when he talks." Frank spun the coin on the night table.

"Do you think this one is his?"

"Hard to tell. But they *are* rare now." Frank shrugged.

"Why don't we just confront him with it? We don't have to mention the spider. Just ask him if this is his silver dollar, and see what he says."

Frank nodded. "Yeah. And we'll watch how he reacts."

"Great," Joe agreed. "When we go downstairs for dinner we'll act as if nothing has happened."

"I can hardly wait to see the look on Peevey's face," Joe said.

They each took a long, hot shower and dressed carefully, wearing ties and jackets for dinner. They checked to see if Iola was okay before descending the highly polished staircase to the hall.

Mr. Peevey was at his usual place, behind the counter, reading. They walked across the Oriental rug in the center of the room and stood at the counter. "Ahem!" Frank cleared his throat loudly.

Peevey spun around on his stool, startled.

He sighed deeply. "Oh, it's you boys!" He seemed surprised to see them. "You certainly move around quietly!"

Frank and Joe simply smiled. Moving silently was part of the training their father had given them. It was second nature to them.

"We didn't mean to frighten you," Joe said with mock sincerity. "It's not nice being frightened."

Peevey appeared flustered. He coughed slightly and said, "Well, what can I do for you boys?"

Frank reached into his pocket and pretended to have difficulty finding what he was looking for.

47

"We found something while we were unpacking," he said, producing the coin. He held the silver dollar level with Peevey's face. "We were wondering if this was yours?"

Peevey's eyes widened for a moment. He took the silver dollar and examined it carefully. Then he said with some certainty, "I do believe it is mine." He felt inside his own pocket and came up empty. "Must be mine! Where on earth did you find it?"

Frank watched Peevey closely and said, "In our room. I found it under my bed."

Peevey's eyes flickered with momentary confusion. He began spinning the coin. "I don't recall —that is, I must have dropped it when I came up to do a room check."

"A room check?" Joe asked.

Peevey smiled. "That's one of my many duties. I have to check the rooms to make certain the maid has done them properly. Sometimes they forget things. You know, like towels or soap."

"Or chocolates," said Frank, watching him closely.

Peevey's eyes darted up. "Or chocolates! Right! They're always forgetting the chocolates. You've found yours, haven't you?"

"Oh, we saw them all right," Frank said grimly. "As a matter of fact, I've already opened mine. But there was one piece missing. I guess the spider must have been hungry!"

Peevey began to spin the coin faster. "Spider? What spider?"

"The spider in the box," Joe stated flatly.

Round and round the coin went. Peevey finally managed a chuckle. "Now let me get this straight. You're saying that instead of one piece of candy in the box, you found a black spider?"

Both Hardys nodded and Frank said, "It fell out and landed on my arm. Good thing it wasn't poisonous!"

Peevey's mouth fell slack and remained in that position briefly. "I can't imagine how it could have gotten there," he finally managed to say, never meeting their eyes, never even looking up. "It's possible that a spider could have gotten into the box at the candy factory, I suppose."

Joe shook his head. "I don't think it could have survived all that time."

"Honestly, I'm at a loss," Peevey said. "I'm sorry. Truly I am, but I have no idea how a spider could have gotten in the box!"

The silver dollar continued to spin and catch the light, throwing it back against the wall.

Frank and Joe glanced at each other. "Well,

thank you, Mr. Peevey," Frank said. "I suppose we'll just have to chalk it up to a strange quirk of nature."

"Spiders and other insects have been known to survive under worse conditions." Peevey smiled.

The Hardys nodded and left him at the counter spinning his silver dollar.

"What do you think?" Joe asked.

"Amazing how Peevey knew the spider was black," said Frank with a raised eyebrow.

Joe smiled. "That's right! We never mentioned the color!"

After the boys spent a few minutes in the parlor talking with the guests, dinner was announced. They followed the others down the hallway to the rear of the inn, where the kitchen and dining room were located.

Place cards had been distributed around the table to indicate where each guest should sit. Frank and Joe found their names and took their seats. Iola's place card was at an empty place beside them. According to their plan, she was to enter a bit late so that all the guests would notice the diamond necklace she was wearing.

"So far so good," Frank mumbled to Joe.

As the waitress began serving the appetizers, Iola made her appearance. "Oh, there you are," she said. "Sorry I'm late, but I had trouble with the clasp on my necklace!"

All the guests' heads turned to look at her. Matt Spyle jumped up first and politely held Iola's chair for her.

Julie's eyes widened at the sight of the necklace, and then she quickly looked down at her food. Brad Wilcox was the only one who didn't notice Iola. He was more engrossed in his own image in the mirror on the wall opposite him.

"Thank you, Matt." Iola smiled graciously. She almost cooed. "You're a perfect gentleman. Not like some brothers I know!" She glared down at Joe and Frank, who sheepishly continued eating their appetizers.

Once she was seated beside him, Joe said loudly, so everyone could hear, "You know you shouldn't have brought that necklace. Mom'll have a fit."

"Don't be silly," Iola said. "Diamonds are meant to be worn. What good are they stuck away in the safe at home?"

Joe sighed, shook his head, and continued eating.

Suddenly, Frank stood up, clutching his throat. "Help me! I can't breathe!" he gasped.

6 An Unexpected Mystery

With lightning speed, Joe laid Frank on the floor and began administering mouth-to-mouth resuscitation. At the same time Iola phoned for the doctor whose number was listed on a card beside the telephone.

Thanks to Joe's quick thinking and action, Frank was breathing normally by the time the doctor arrived. At the doctor's request, Brad and Joe carried Frank into the parlor. Then Brad returned to the dining room.

After examining Frank and asking him some questions, Dr. Hawkins said, "I'd say this was nothing more than an asthma attack."

Joe looked confused. Frank managed to sit up. "Asthma! I've never even had a *hint* of it!"

Dr. Hawkins shrugged. "You never know about these things. Anything could bring it on—the rind of a cheese, anything. You're sure you didn't choke?"

Frank shook his head and lay back down. "No, I didn't choke. All of a sudden, my windpipe just closed up."

The doctor appeared puzzled. "If you like, we can go to the emergency room and run a few tests."

Frank declined. "Thanks anyway, but I feel fine now."

Dr. Hawkins closed his bag, smiled, and said, "I'm sure you'll be all right. If you have any more problems, give me a call."

As the doctor closed the parlor door behind him, Frank turned to Joe and said, "I think someone tampered with my food."

Joe agreed. "You *were* fine until you started eating the appetizer. Funny, it didn't affect me at all."

"I know there are certain drugs that can constrict your throat, causing an asthmalike attack!"

"Too bad there was none of your food left," Joe said. "We could have had some tests run on it."

Frank sat up on the sofa. "But I didn't eat it all! What happened to it?"

Joe let out a deep breath. "In all the confusion, your plate was removed from the table."

"That proves it," cried Frank. "My food was tampered with! Someone is trying to cover their tracks! No question about it."

Just then, Chet walked into the room. Since they were pretending to be strangers, he had to act as though he didn't know them. "Hi, I'm Chet Morton," he said. "I saw them carry you into the parlor here. You gave us quite a scare back in the dining room. Are you okay now?"

Joe knew that Chet had been worried sick about his friend but was sticking to his role as planned.

Frank smiled. "I'm fine. My name's Frank Hardy, and this is my brother, Joe."

For the benefit of anyone who might be looking in from the hall, they all shook hands as if for the first time.

"If there's anything I can do, just let me know," Chet said. "Meanwhile, I think I'll return to the dining room and finish dinner. You fellows up to joining me?"

Joe looked at his brother and raised an eyebrow. "Feel like eating anything, Frank?"

"I've sort of lost my appetite," he replied.

"That's what I figured," Joe said. "But we do

have to eat. I don't think anyone would try anything again so soon."

Frank took a deep breath. "I suppose you're right. I'll just be careful, that's all."

Joe was suddenly serious. "We'll *all* be careful."

They returned to the dining room just as the rest of the guests were starting their dessert. No one else had gotten ill. After assuring everyone that he was all right, Frank took his seat next to Joe.

"Thank goodness you're all right," Iola said.

The other guests nodded in agreement and the waitress quickly served them their main course.

As they enjoyed their meal, Frank and Joe were alert. They watched each guest carefully, trying to come up with incriminating clues—for the fake mystery—based on each person's individual quirks.

Matt Spyle turned out to be pretty quiet. He even read a mystery novel while he ate his dessert.

"He's either very rude or a nut about mysteries," Frank whispered to Joe after Matt had excused himself.

Joe smiled. "He doesn't mean to be rude. I

think he's just wrapped up in his own world."

After dinner the Hardys—and Chet, who'd asked for seconds on dessert—joined the other guests in the parlor. The television set had been turned on. Brad and Julie, who were getting along very well, sat together on the couch watching an old movie. Frank, Joe, Chet, and Iola hung out for part of it. The older people went to bed early. Finally Frank said, "Well, it's been a long day. I think I'll go upstairs and get a good night's sleep."

Julie seemed miffed. "Some mystery weekend! So far, the only mystery we've seen has been on television."

Frank looked at Joe in amazement. Julie had no way of knowing what they'd been through in the past few hours!

"Give it time," Frank said to Julie. "I'm sure the management of the Sky Blue Inn has all sorts of things planned for us."

"I wish they'd get on with it." She snorted. "I'm bored!"

Brad interrupted her. "You're bored? With me sitting beside you? I'm crushed!"

"I'm not bored with you," Julie said, smiling sweetly at him. "It's just that I paid for a mystery weekend, and I expect—"

"You expect what?" Brad asked. "Bodies to fall

out of closets? An ax murderer on the loose? What?"

"Oh, I don't know. Just—something. Actually, anything."

Frank cut in. "I think the management is doing a good job, Julie. You don't know what to expect! Isn't that what a mystery is supposed to be?"

Julie thought for a minute. "I see what you mean. All this waiting is kind of suspenseful!"

Frank grinned. "Then the mystery has already started," he said. "It's not just a question of *what* will happen—but *when.*"

With that, Frank and Joe excused themselves and went upstairs to their room.

Frank removed his jacket and hung it up. "Tomorrow the fun starts, when Iola's necklace disappears. Did you see the way everyone looked at it? In the dining-room candlelight, it sure looked real."

Joe nodded. "We've set them up perfectly, even if I do say so—"

His words were cut off by a scream from the hallway.

"Iola!" Joe tore open the door, and he and Frank charged into the hall. Julie was backing away from her room, a trembling hand to her mouth. When she saw them, she rushed headlong into Frank's arms.

"Th-there's someone in my room," she whispered.

"Are you sure?" asked Frank.

"Positive!" Julie's voice was a little steadier now. "When I unlocked my door, I saw someone moving around, outlined against the window."

"Let's go then. But you stay behind us," cautioned Frank. On the thick Oriental runner, he and Joe stole soundlessly toward Julie's room. The room was dark. Frightened by the intruder, Julie hadn't taken the time to turn on the lights.

The Hardys stood for a second beside the door, not moving. Slipping his hand around the doorjamb, Frank felt the wall for the light switch. He flicked it on, and they rushed inside.

Empty! But Julie's room was a wreck. The drawers had been pulled out of the dresser and lay overturned on the floor. Her luggage was strewn about, the contents spilled all across the bed.

"Nobody's here now, but it looks like your room was hit by a small tornado," Joe said. "Somebody really went through your stuff!"

"And whoever it was, he was in a big hurry," Frank commented. "You must have scared him when you put your key in the lock."

Julie stood motionless, her hand over her

58

mouth. She was in shock. "I can't believe it!" she finally managed to say.

"You'd better go through everything and see if anything is missing," suggested Frank. "Joe and I will check the room for clues."

As they began looking, they heard a low moan from Julie. "Oh, no, my watch is gone! And my camera, too!"

Frank rushed to her side. "You're sure?"

Julie searched frantically. "I left them on top of the dresser. Now they're gone!"

She sat down on the edge of the bed and began to cry. Frank put his hand on her shoulder to comfort her. "We'll find out who did this. And we'll get your stuff back, too," he promised.

Joe shouted from the bathroom. "Frank! Come here, quick!"

Frank rushed into the bathroom to join his brother, who was kneeling beside the bathtub. "Look at the footprints on the bottom of the tub!"

Frank bent down and examined the prints carefully. "These shoes had rubber soles—and look at that waffle-grid pattern. It's really unusual."

Joe pointed above the tub. "The window is open."

"That must be how the thief made his escape," Frank guessed.

"But we're on the second floor."

"Look out the window and see if you can spot a way down."

Joe pulled himself up on the windowsill and peered out into the darkness. "Bingo. There's a drainpipe right next to the window, and part of a print on the ledge outside!"

"Let's get downstairs fast," said Frank, moving toward the door.

Joe joined his brother in the hall, and they headed for the stairs. Julie stayed behind to straighten up her room.

The boys raced out the front entrance of the inn and around to the side of the building just below Julie's window. As they neared the spot beneath the drainpipe, they slowed their pace.

"Careful now," Frank said. "We don't want to disturb any footprints."

"It's too dark to see anything," said Joe.

"Just a minute." Frank fumbled in his pocket for his pen flashlight. "Look!" Frank pointed to some footprints visible in the soft earth beneath the drainpipe. "The same pattern."

Joe whistled. "We came up here to stage a mystery, and now we're smack in the middle of a real one!"

"Sure looks that way," Frank agreed. "This whole thing is getting weirder and weirder."

They slowly began following the footprints away from the inn, stopping frequently to check on the trail.

Suddenly there was a crackling in the bushes nearby. "Shh!" Frank grabbed Joe's arm and held him back. He pocketed his flashlight. "We've got company!"

A figure rose up from the tangle of branches and bolted across the grounds. Frank and Joe took off in hot pursuit. Leaping hedges and flower beds, they could barely keep the figure in sight.

"He's going for the parking lot!" shouted Frank, running next to his brother.

The Hardys quickened their pace and gained a few steps on their quarry. He sprinted past the parking lot and headed toward the woods beyond the inn.

"We've got to catch him before he loses us!" cried Frank. Their lungs were burning, but they managed to pump one last burst of speed into their weary legs. They caught up with the runner just before he slipped into the darkness of the trees.

Frank dove and brought the running figure down with a flying tackle.

Standing up to confront the thief, Frank was hit in the shoulder with a powerful kick that slammed him back against a tree.

His opponent was well trained—and fighting for his life!

7 The Game Is Afoot

The force of the blow momentarily knocked the wind out of Frank. Out of the corner of his eye he saw another kick coming, but managed to roll out of the way before it landed. When he rose to his feet again, he threw an uppercut that almost lifted the intruder off his feet.

It was pitch dark, making it difficult for Joe to help his brother. He finally managed to grab hold of the culprit from behind, but was rewarded with an elbow in the stomach.

For a moment the brothers thought they had lost the stranger—till Frank turned and saw the dark figure hurtling straight for him. Frank neatly sidestepped, thrust out his foot, and brought his attacker crashing to the ground. Both Hardys pounced on him.

The trio rolled in the grass and leaves with fists flying until, at last, Joe Hardy pinned the culprit in a wrestling hold that was unbreakable.

Hauling him to his feet, they shoved their captive ahead of them until they came to the lighted area of the parking lot. Once there, they pushed him against a car and spun him around.

It was Matt Spyle!

"Matt!" exclaimed Joe. He was amazed at the physical strength of the skinny young man.

"Okay, you've got some explaining to do," Frank said through gritted teeth.

"About what?" Matt asked blankly. "Maybe you have some explaining to do, too."

"If you don't mind, we'll ask the questions. Why'd you break into Julie's room and steal her watch and camera?" Joe asked.

"What are you talking about?" asked Matt.

Frank let out a deep breath. "Why were you hiding in the bushes?"

"And why did you run away from us?" asked Joe.

"Why did you chase me?" Matt replied. "I haven't done anything! I was out jogging, and was on my way back to the inn when I noticed two people checking out the grounds. I was about to identify myself, but then I realized you might be burglars, so I decided just to slip away quietly and not get involved. But I stepped on a dry twig or something, and you heard me. I panicked and ran! I'm a fast runner, and I thought I could get away, but you guys are faster." Matt paused and then continued. "Anyway, when you caught me, I fought back. I've been trained in karate, you know."

Frank rubbed his sore shoulders. "Yes, we noticed."

"You put up quite a fight for someone who claims to be innocent," said Joe.

"That was pure reflex," Matt explained. "Look, if I were the thief, wouldn't I have the loot on me?"

Joe shrugged. "He's right. We haven't exactly caught him with the goods."

"He could have stashed it somewhere and planned to come back for it later," suggested Frank.

Matt interrupted them. "I know it looks bad," he said. "But if it's any help, I did see someone else on that side of the inn shortly before you two came out."

Frank's eyes widened. "Can you describe that someone?"

Matt sighed. "I was afraid you'd ask that. No,

not really. It's awfully dark out here. All I know for sure is he was a lot bigger than I am."

"Excuse us for a moment." Frank pulled his brother aside.

"I'm not going anywhere," said Matt. He leaned back against the car while the Hardys held their conference.

"What do you think?" Frank whispered to Joe.

"I think he might be trying to pull a fast one on us," Joe whispered back. "That stuff about seeing someone running away from the inn could be a cover."

"True," agreed Frank. "And that little-shy-guy routine could be part of it." Frank sighed. "Then again, he might be telling the truth."

They both glanced back at Matt, who was quietly waiting for them.

"There's one way to find out," Frank said decisively.

The Hardys moved back to their prisoner. Frank looked him coldly in the eye and said, "Matt, lift up your foot!"

Matt appeared confused. "Why?"

"Go ahead, Matt," Joe said. "Just lift up your foot! Is that such a big deal?"

"No," complained Matt. "It just doesn't make much sense to me." He hesitated, but when he saw the determined looks in the Hardys' eyes, he

66

knew they both meant business. He slowly lifted his right foot.

"Higher," ordered Frank. "Tilt it toward the lamppost so it catches the light."

Matt tilted his foot, and the sole of his shoe was bathed in soft yellow light. The Hardys had the proof they needed!

The sole of Matt's shoe had a distinct waffle-grid pattern.

The Hardys looked at each other and then turned their gaze on Matt. "I'm afraid you have a lot of explaining to do," Frank said seriously.

Matt looked astonished. "What do you mean?"

"The soles of your shoes match the prints we found in Julie's bathroom," said Frank.

"And the prints on the ground just under her window," Joe added.

Panic filled Matt's eyes. "It wasn't me, I tell you! Prints or no prints, I've never been in Julie's room. And I've never been outside her window!"

Joe looked at him sadly. "Matt, you're expecting us to believe a lot."

"I'm not trying to pull anything!" cried Matt.

Frank took Matt by the arm. "Okay! There's one more thing we can do. If that checks out, then you've had it."

They marched Matt across the grounds and back to the area beneath Julie's window. When they reached the spot they were looking for, Frank pulled out his penlight. The footprints were revealed in the smoky glow. "Put your foot beside that print. Come on, now!"

Matt took a deep breath, lifted his right foot, and placed it down on the ground beside the footprint.

The print made by the thief was much bigger.

He breathed a sigh of relief. "I told you I saw someone bigger than me running away from here."

Frank and Joe looked at each other. The burglar was still out there somewhere!

8 Planting Clues

Frank and Joe were up early on Saturday morning. Both brothers had always been early risers, especially when they were working on a case. Now they wanted to set their plans in motion while the guests slept.

They dressed quickly, and quietly stepped into the hall outside their room. No one else was around.

"So far, so good," Joe whispered as they eased toward the stairs.

Frank smiled. "The early bird catches the worm or, in this case, gets to plant the clues," he whispered back.

Frank and Joe sneaked silently down the long

stairs. When they reached the lobby, they were glad to see that Mr. Peevey wasn't at his post.

Once outside, the boys got in their van and sped off to a nearby village mall. On the way, they compared their notes on the guests.

"What did you come up with, Joe?" Frank asked.

"I noticed that Brad Wilcox is always chewing gum, so I made a point of finding out what brand. It's called Triple Mint. We can pick up a pack of that," Joe said.

"That's easy." Frank smiled. "Iola told me the kind of perfume Julie wears. It's called Reuben."

"Reuben?" Joe grinned. "You mean Julie wears a perfume that smells like a sandwich? Chet'd love that!"

Frank laughed. "Anyway, Iola said we can pick up a bottle at any drugstore."

"What about Matt Spyle?"

Frank hesitated for a moment. "I'm not sure we should plant clues incriminating Matt. Especially after what we put him through last night."

"I know," Joe said. "But he really did look guilty until those footprints cleared him."

"So what should we do? Do you think he'd like to be one of our main suspects?"

Joe grinned. "Yeah, I think so. He loves mysteries. If we left him out, he'd be hurt."

"You're right," Frank agreed. "So what clue can we plant about him?"

Joe thought for a moment. "He's always reading a paperback mystery. And I noticed he writes his name in ink on the inside cover. Like we used to do when we were kids. You know, 'This book belongs to,' and then his name!"

Frank chuckled. "He does that?"

"Yeah," replied Joe. "He seems to be very protective of his books. So I thought I'd 'borrow' one and plant it as a clue."

"Great! Anyone else? Or do you think three main suspects are enough?" Frank asked.

"Any more people and it gets too confusing."

They pulled into the mall and parked in front of a large drugstore. It didn't take them long to find the things they needed to put their mystery weekend in high gear.

Back in the van, Frank took the wheel, and Joe asked, "Now that we have our 'clues,' just exactly what are we going to do with them?"

"Plant them in Iola's room, of course," Frank said. He glanced down at his watch. "Iola is going to rush into the dining room at lunch and scream that her necklace has been stolen. So we've got three hours."

"It shouldn't take more than a few minutes," said Joe.

"Right. So let's head back." Frank started the van. "We wouldn't want any of the guests to start wondering later why we'd missed breakfast."

As they drove toward the inn, they discussed how they were going to set up the guests.

"This is going to be great!" Frank said. "In no time at all, they're going to be accusing each other!"

Suddenly, Joe remembered something. "Hey, we're going to have to plant one more clue—for Chet."

"I've already thought of that," Frank said. "And guess what the clue involves?"

"Um—could it possibly have something to do with food?" Joe asked innocently.

"Right you are," said Frank with a broad grin.

"But who's going to discover all this?"

"Depends on what kind of detectives the guests turn out to be. And while they're trying to solve our mystery, we have a bit of detecting to do ourselves. With all the fun we're having, we almost forgot the real burglary."

"It should work out well. Everyone will think we're trying to find Iola's necklace, while we're really looking for Julie's camera and watch." Joe frowned. "Hey, a thought just occurred to me. What if the guests don't solve the mystery?"

"Then we'll have to do it for them," replied Frank. "But I hope someone solves it. It'll be more fun that way."

"So if everything works out," Joe said, "Chet will break down and confess when he's confronted. I hope the mystery lasts until Sunday at noon. If it looks as if someone is getting too close, too soon, we might have to plant more clues."

"Here we are," Frank interrupted as they pulled in the driveway. "Let's go catch a burglar!"

Peevey stepped out from the lobby to greet them when they came through the front door. "Out early, eh, fellows?"

"Uh-huh, we had to pick up a few things," said Joe.

Peevey smiled indulgently. "Tourists must have their souvenirs."

Frank and Joe laughed. "Now how did you guess we were out souvenir hunting?" Frank asked.

"It's what all the guests do eventually," replied Peevey smugly. "I'm very observant."

Frank winked at Joe. "I can certainly believe that. Nothing gets past you, right, Mr. Peevey?"

The Hardys both chuckled as they walked away. Joe went upstairs to drop off their purchases in their room. Frank headed for the dining room. About halfway there he stopped and called back to Peevey, "By the way, has Mr. Maxwell shown up yet?"

Peevey smiled. "No, he's still out of town. I don't expect him this weekend."

After breakfast Frank and Joe returned to their room. They waited a few minutes, then crossed the hall and knocked softly on Iola's door. She opened it cautiously. "Come in, quick!" she whispered.

As they entered, Frank noticed Brad standing in the doorway of his room, watching them.

Closing the door behind him, Frank said, "Brad saw us come in here."

Joe shrugged. "That's okay. Iola's supposed to be our sister. I don't think he'll find anything funny about it."

Frank opened the bag he was carrying and explained to Iola what they were going to do.

"Great!" Iola said when he finished explaining. The three of them quickly set up her room for the discovery of the theft.

"Okay, let's head downstairs," Frank said. "One more person to frame."

As they walked toward the lobby they saw Matt in the parlor, reading. They passed by. When they reached the sitting room, Joe turned to Frank and said, "Try to get him outside for some reason so we can 'borrow' his book."

Frank walked back to the parlor, poked his head inside, and said, "Matt, can I see you for a minute?"

Matt looked surprised, then slightly fearful. "Sure." He put his book down on the table beside the chair and followed Frank out the door.

"Let's go check those footprints again," Frank said. "We may have missed something."

Matt was uneasy. "Okay, but they were too big to be made by my feet, remember?"

"Relax," Frank said. "You're in the clear." The two of them disappeared outside.

With Matt out of the way, Joe slipped into the parlor and pocketed his book. As he did, he spotted Julie passing by. He darted back into the hallway and hurried after her. "Hi, Julie!" he said, hoping she hadn't seen him in the parlor.

Julie looked at him suspiciously. "Hi, Joe. Having a busy morning?"

"Very busy," Joe explained. "Frank and I went down to the village early this morning to do some shopping. How are you feeling today?"

Julie smiled knowingly. "Much better, now that our mystery weekend has begun."

Joe looked surprised. He wondered if she'd caught on to what he and Frank were up to. "What do you mean?" he asked.

"I'm talking about the—quote—robbery in my room last night." Julie grinned. "Having someone *pretend* to rob my room is the official beginning of the weekend. I'm so excited! I can hardly wait to see what happens next!"

With that, she went outside. Joe was still standing there, staring after her, when Frank came up behind him. He'd come back inside through the kitchen door.

"She doesn't believe her room was really robbed," Joe exclaimed with surprise.

Frank let out a deep breath. "Well, would you if you were at a mystery weekend and your room was burgled? It's better this way. At least she's not upset anymore, and it'll give us time to catch the real thief!" He looked carefully at Joe. "Didn't you get it?"

Joe grinned. "Don't worry. I've got it. Where's Matt?"

"I left him outside, searching for clues. He's really eager to help."

"Who knows? He might come up with something."

The boys went outside to plant the last clue.

When they returned, they overheard Brad and Julie talking in the parlor and stopped to listen.

"I don't trust those Hardys," Brad was saying.

"Neither do I," agreed Julie. "I saw them slip out early this morning, and they were being awfully quiet. Innocent people don't sneak around like that."

Brad nodded. "They acted really suspiciously when they went into Iola's room after breakfast. Kept looking around like they were afraid they were being watched. You know, this weekend could just be a cover for a real robbery. The Hardys could be behind it all!"

Julie gasped. "I hadn't thought of that! Do you think they actually stole my stuff?"

Brad answered with a shrug.

Frank and Joe couldn't believe what they were hearing. Frank began to laugh. "It's a good thing we're not thieves," he whispered. "We're not cut out to be crooks."

"I'm going to go up to the room for a minute before lunch," Joe called over his shoulder, already taking the stairs two at a time.

He raced down the hall along the narrow strip of patterned carpet. Just before the door to their room, he stopped. That's funny, I know I locked the room, he thought. Then he heard whistling, and saw the maid at the far end of the hall. Joe smiled. She must have forgotten to lock the door after she'd cleaned their room.

He pushed the door open with his fingertips and stepped over the threshold into the room. In the next second he felt a blinding pain explode in his head and suddenly the floor rushed up to meet him!

9 The Phony Crime

Chet looked at his watch and rubbed his hands together. "It's almost noon. They'll be serving lunch in ten minutes."

"Then it'll be time for Iola to play her greatest role." Frank chuckled, but his expression quickly changed. "Hmm, I wonder what's keeping Joe. It's been ten minutes since he went upstairs. Did you see him come down?"

"Nope. Do you want me to go up and check on him?" Chet asked.

"No, I'll go," Frank said, feeling a quick tightening in his stomach. He took a deep breath to calm himself and marched up the stairs. At the landing he saw an open door—207—his room!

He raced inside and almost tripped over his brother's prone body.

Frank's mouth fell open when he saw Joe's shirt. Scrawled in Magic Marker were the words: "Get out and go home!"

"Oooh," Joe groaned, and tried to sit up.

"No, no. Lie still, Joe. Don't move."

"I'll feel better if I get up. Just give me a hand," Joe said.

"Okay, but do it slowly. It looks like someone hit you pretty hard on the back of the head. Did you see who did it?"

"No, I walked in and saw nothing but stars until I came to and looked up into your beautiful brown eyes," Joe said, fluttering his eyelashes.

"Now I know you're all right. Another comment like that and I'll personally send you back to starland. Here"—Frank grabbed his brother's arm—"let's see if I can hoist you up."

On his feet again, Joe asked Frank not to tell anyone about the attack. "If the culprit is at lunch, I don't want to give him—or her—the satisfaction of getting a reaction from me."

"Are you sure you don't want to rest for a while?"

"Positive." After Joe changed his shirt, the brothers went down to find all the guests but Iola seated in the dining room. Frank and Joe took their seats and listened to Julie, who was talking excitedly.

"Our mystery weekend has finally begun," Julie was telling the others. "Last night my room was ransacked, and my camera and watch were taken. Now it's up to us to solve it!"

"How do you know it wasn't a real robbery?" asked Matt, looking concerned. "Someone stole one of my books from under my nose!"

"Someone probably just borrowed your book, Matt. Or maybe they thought it belonged to the inn. A book for the guests to read."

Matt snorted. "My name was clearly written on the inside cover."

"I'm sure it'll turn up," said Julie, dismissing him with a wave of her hand. Matt turned sullen and began picking at his food. "Anyway," Julie said, continuing, "I think we should all begin looking for clues. Joe and Frank have found some already."

Frank coughed. "Yes, we found some footprints." He didn't mention the waffle-grid sole marks because they were a clue in the real robbery.

Just then Iola burst into the room looking terrified. "My necklace has been stolen!" she cried. "Someone's been in my room," she said, turning to Frank. "And Grandma's diamond necklace is gone!"

Frank helped her along with the story. "Iola, are you sure you just didn't misplace it? You know how you always lose things."

She gave him a look of annoyance. "I wouldn't misplace Grandma's antique necklace. You know it's worth thousands!"

"I can't believe it. We told you not to bring it. Well, when did you last see it?" asked Joe.

"I checked it this morning. It was in the top drawer of my dresser—in a box under some socks. When I got back from a walk, the door to my room was open, the drawer had been pulled out, the socks were on the floor, and the necklace was gone!" She buried her face in her hands and sobbed.

Julie clapped her hands gleefully. "This is great! The mystery is getting better and better! Now we've got two robberies to solve!"

Iola looked up, astonished. "You mean you think this is just part of the mystery weekend?"

"Of course!" Julie's eyes flashed with excitement. "These robberies were set up for us to solve! So we'd better get busy."

Iola looked at Frank and Joe, and managed to

give them a wink. Their plan was working perfectly.

Everyone gobbled up their food and headed upstairs to investigate Iola's room. Frank and Joe watched with amusement as the guests began to play detective.

In Iola's room, they all began searching for clues. "Don't touch anything," Frank said. "If you find anything, just leave it where it is. We don't want to disturb any evidence. For all we know, this could be a real robbery!"

"Do you really think so?" Matt asked eagerly.

"There've been a lot of hotel robberies in this area," Joe explained. "The thieves could be using this mystery weekend as a cover for a real robbery."

Brad looked up. "That's exactly what I was telling Julie earlier. Only I have some suspects in mind."

"Really?" Frank challenged. "Who?"

"I'm not saying"—Brad smirked—"until I'm ready."

Frank glanced at Joe and rolled his eyes.

"Well, well, look here," said Matt. He held up a Triple Mint gum wrapper. "Anyone ever see this before?"

Brad spoke up. "Of course! That's a very popular brand of gum."

Matt gave him a suspicious look. "Yes, but you're the only one in this crowd who chews it. In fact, you chew and pop it constantly. It gets on my nerves."

"So I chew Triple Mint." Brad snorted. "That doesn't make me a thief!"

"Then what is this wrapper doing in Iola's room?" Matt asked triumphantly. "Iola, did you invite Brad to your room?"

Iola looked shocked. "Of course not! I hardly know him."

Matt held up the ashtray. "Look! Gum in the ashtray. Such a nasty habit!"

Brad was furious. "If you don't stop making remarks, I'm going to punch you out!"

Matt smiled knowingly. "I wish you'd try!"

Frank and Joe could barely keep from laughing out loud. Brad had no way of knowing that skinny little Matt was a martial-arts expert.

Brad backed away from the group as if he were under attack. "All I know is, I've never been inside this room before now! Somebody planted that stuff here to throw the blame on me!"

"Brad's right. The thief could have planted that gum wrapper to throw us off. Let's see if we can find any more clues," Chet said to break the tension.

The guests returned to snooping. Suddenly

84

Iola grabbed Chet and pulled him away from her closet. "What are you doing, going through my things?"

"Just looking for clues, like everyone else," Chet explained, playing along with her game.

"If anyone goes through my clothes, it'll be me," snapped Iola. She began pushing clothes hangers back on the rack. Then she stopped suddenly, sniffed, and pulled out her coat. She held it up to her nose and sniffed again.

"My coat reeks of perfume! And it's not mine!"

Brad reached out. "Let me smell." He held the coat close to his face. "I'd recognize that perfume anywhere. It's the one that Julie uses."

Julie gasped. "W-what?"

Brad held out Iola's coat for her. "Go ahead. Take a whiff. I'm sure you'll recognize it! You're the only one here who wears this stuff!"

Julie took the coat and sniffed. "It's Reuben!"

Iola stood with her hands on her hips. "And I don't wear Reuben! Julie, you've been in my room trying on my coat!"

Matt stepped forward. "Yeah. And what else did you do while you were in here? Did you just happen to walk out with Iola's grandmother's necklace?"

Julie stepped back, her hand to her mouth. "Now, wait a minute! You don't think that I—"

Matt moved in for the kill. "I'll bet you even *staged* that robbery in your own room to make us think you were a victim, too! Very clever, Julie. But not quite clever enough!"

Frank laughed under his breath and wondered which old mystery show Matt had gotten that line from.

Julie was shocked. "You can't believe that I'd do something like that! I was robbed, honestly! Just ask Frank and Joe. They know. They were there!"

Brad's eyebrows went up. "Oh! They were there?"

"They came running in just after I discovered someone had been in my room!"

"What does that prove? And how do we know one of them isn't guilty?" Brad asked, eyes wide.

"I—I don't know," Julie stammered. "I—I don't know what to believe anymore!"

Frank interrupted them. "It looks like we're all suspects."

Joe backed him up. "It's true. Someone in this room has to be a thief."

"Even you, Matt," Iola said. "I saw you sneaking around the grounds late last night just after Julie's robbery. What were *you* doing out then?"

Matt looked annoyed. "I always jog at least three miles a day. Last night I remembered I hadn't gotten around to it, so I ran before going to bed."

Frank said, "He's telling the truth. When we went outside, we met him. He had just been out jogging."

"Oh, yeah?" Brad said. "Anyone can say he was jogging. And how do we know the three of you aren't in this together? You could have planned the whole thing."

Frank held up a hand. "Wait a minute! We aren't going to get anywhere if we go around accusing each other without proof."

"Yeah," agreed Julie. "If the Sky Blue Inn planned this mystery, then one of their employees is probably involved."

"Like Mr. Peevey," suggested Matt. "Or even Botts!"

"Botts looks like he'd be capable of anything," said Iola.

Julie nodded. "I don't trust him one bit."

Frank and Joe both stifled grins. It was going even better than they'd planned! The guests were accusing one another—and now the staff of the inn!

Iola cornered Julie. "That still doesn't explain why you broke into my room and tried on my coat!"

Julie lost her cool. "I didn't break into your

room! And I haven't been near your stupid coat!" she shouted.

"Hold it, hold it!" Joe ordered. "Simmer down!"

"She has no right accusing me," Julie said, her voice a little quieter.

"There's no reason to lose your temper. This is supposed to be fun."

Julie looked embarrassed. "I'm sorry, but I don't know what's real and what's fake anymore! I don't know what to believe!"

Frank smiled. "Remember when you were complaining about being bored? How do you feel now?"

Julie blushed. "Not bored," she said sheepishly.

"That's the point," Frank remarked.

"I suppose you're right. We sure are getting our money's worth."

Iola spoke up. "If you're through searching my room, I'd appreciate it if you'd all leave."

"Testy, testy," said Brad as he started to follow the others out.

"Back off, Brad," Joe said. "She's upset."

"Who appointed you leader?"

"I'm not, I'm just her brother," said Joe.

"Flake," Brad muttered under his breath, and left the room.

Joe spoke to Iola so the others could overhear in the hallway. "I just don't understand why you didn't put Grandma's necklace in the safe. You know how Mom and Dad feel about it."

When the last footstep in the hall had receded, Iola whispered to Joe, "How'd I do?"

"Terrific!" Joe said. "We've got them all fighting, and nobody trusts anybody!"

Just then Peevey came scurrying down the hall. "Has anyone seen Mr. Botts?" His voice was high and shrill.

"Botts?" asked Frank. "Last time we saw him, he was downstairs."

"I've got to find him quickly!" cried Peevey, his ferret eyes shifting nervously. "The office safe has been robbed!"

10 A Real Crime

Mr. Botts lumbered up the stairs as Peevey, Frank, and Joe were about to scramble down. "What is it, Mr. Peevey?"

"The office safe has been opened!" Peevey clutched the big man by the shoulders and desperately looked into his eyes. "The lock was picked—all the weekend proceeds and the guests' valuables have been stolen!"

Without saying a word, Botts turned and ran down the stairs faster than Frank or Joe thought possible for such a big man. Peevey and the boys followed close behind.

They trotted across the lobby and into the small office. Against the back wall was a chunky black safe, about three feet high. The door was standing wide open.

"Mr. Maxwell's going to give me the ax when he finds out about this," moaned Peevey, wringing his hands.

Frank and Joe knelt beside Botts and peered inside the safe.

"They sure cleaned it out." Joe whistled as he spoke.

"Why 'they'?" asked Botts.

Joe looked flustered for a moment. "I don't know—it just came out of my mouth."

Botts eyed him carefully. Then he said, "Two people had to do it!" He was staring straight at Frank and Joe.

Just then there was a commotion in the doorway. When they looked around, they saw Julie, Matt, Brad, and Iola staring bug-eyed at the empty safe.

Julie finally broke the silence. "This is great! One mystery piled on top of another!"

Botts stood up and spoke more than he had all weekend. "If you think this is part of the mystery weekend, think again. We've got a serious crime on our hands! Nobody is to leave the premises until we get to the bottom of this. I'm calling the police!"

While Botts reached for the phone, Brad crossed toward the safe and knelt down beside Frank and Joe.

"Don't touch anything," Frank cautioned him. "There might be fingerprints."

Brad shot him an angry glance. "Who do you guys think you are? You're always giving orders, trying to take charge! I'm sick of it!"

"Just trying to help," said Frank, shrugging his shoulders. "You aren't supposed to disturb anything at the scene of a crime." He stood up and backed away a couple of steps.

"You know, I've had it with you!" Brad stormed out of the room.

Frank shook his head. "These thefts are getting on everyone's nerves."

Botts hung up the phone. "The police are coming. Everyone clear out, and don't touch anything!"

Frank saw Brad standing outside. He rolled his eyes when he heard that. "Come on. Move!" said Botts. "Don't hang around the lobby, either. The whole area is off-limits!"

The Hardys and other guests marched across the hall and into the parlor. They all sat in silence, each lost in his or her thoughts.

Finally Julie broke the silence. "That Botts is a

really good actor! The way he acted so angry. He was very convincing!"

Joe leaned toward her. "Julie, I don't think this is part of our mystery."

She scoffed. "Don't tell me that safe robbery was for real!"

Quietly, Frank said, "He called the police, Julie. Doesn't that mean anything to you?"

"The police? They'll probably be some actors from the local community theater group. Actually, I can hardly wait! I bet they'll put on quite a show!"

Matt grinned. "Julie's right. This is all a setup. It's what we paid our money for."

Frank sat back in his chair and let out a deep sigh. He decided to go along with the others. "Okay, I suppose you're right. Let's just sit back and enjoy it!"

"Yeah? Well, I don't think it's a setup. I think you two are in it up to your ears," Brad said, pointing to Joe and Frank. "As far as I'm concerned, we don't have to look any further!"

Frank just smiled at him. "There's just one problem with your theory, Brad."

"What's that?"

"You don't have any proof," Frank said firmly, and stood up and excused himself.

Frank walked into the hall and just missed colliding with Chet. "Frank, Joe? Follow me. Quick!"

Frank asked, "What's up?"

Chet didn't answer. Instead, he headed up the staircase.

"Why are you being so secretive?" Joe asked.

"You'll see. You'll see. Come in my room." Chet opened the door and the Hardys followed him inside.

"Okay, what's up?" Frank asked.

Chet stood in the center of the room. "Notice anything?"

The Hardys' eyes searched the room. There was nothing different about it.

"Smell funny to you?" Chet asked.

"Cigar smoke!" both Hardys exclaimed.

"Smell familiar?"

"Mr. Maxwell!" said Frank.

"Right," agreed Chet. "Remember, back at the mall, when we first met Maxwell, he lit up a cigar that smelled exactly like this."

"You're right. Just like dirty socks! I'd recognize it anywhere," Joe said. "That means Maxwell must be here!"

"If he's here," Frank said, "why doesn't he let us know?"

"And why was he snooping in my room?" Chet asked.

Just then, two police cars roared up the driveway and stopped in front of the inn. The boys looked out the window, the flashing red lights shining on their faces.

Three uniformed police officers and one redheaded man in civilian clothes leapt out and stormed into the lobby. Chet, Frank, and Joe ran out of Chet's room and down the stairs.

"Very impressive," Julie said. "They almost look real."

"Those *are* real patrol cars, Julie," Frank said quietly.

All at once Julie looked confused. "Are—are you sure . . .?"

"Don't tell me you're falling for this farce!" Matt said.

The Hardys left the hall and followed the police into the lobby. Peevey and Botts were in the office.

"Nothing's been touched," Botts was saying. "Everything's exactly as we found it."

Two officers knelt down to examine the safe, while the other two searched the office for clues.

"Looks like a professional job, Sergeant," said

one of the officers as he rose from the safe. He was speaking to the redheaded man in civilian clothes. The plainclothes detective approached the Hardys, who were standing in the doorway. "What are you two doing here?" he said gruffly.

"We're guests of the inn," Frank said. He was about to explain, to tell him exactly who they were, when the officer interrupted.

He identified himself as Detective Sergeant Culp of the local police. "Get back in the parlor with the others. We're coming in later to ask a few questions."

Obediently, the Hardys returned to the parlor. "Let's stay out of the way until we know what's going on," Frank whispered. "We don't want to blow our cover unless it's absolutely necessary."

"I'd feel a lot better if Mr. Maxwell were here," said Joe.

"He must be around somewhere," Frank said. "But why doesn't he make himself known?"

"He's the only person who can prove that we were *hired* to come up here," Joe said.

"Yeah," Frank replied. "Anyway, let's keep cool and do our own investigating."

Back in the parlor, Matt was trying to impress Julie. "Nobody in his right mind would believe those bozos are real police officers!"

Frank and Joe glanced at each other. If the others only knew how real all this was!

Matt went on. "The way they stormed in here, I could tell it was an act."

All at once, the redheaded detective appeared in the doorway. "Don't anybody leave this room. We're going upstairs to have a look around."

"Do you have a search warrant?" asked Brad, half joking. He smiled with superiority.

"Why? Do you have something to hide?" Detective Culp snapped back at him.

The smile left Brad's face. "N-no, officer! Go right ahead!"

The detective wasn't about to let up on him. "We can get a search warrant very quickly if you don't want to cooperate!"

"Feel free to search *my* room," Matt volunteered. "I've got nothing to hide."

"Mine, too," Julie added.

Peevey interrupted. "You have my personal permission to search every room in the inn! I want this matter cleared up as soon as possible!" He stood in the hall, twitching nervously. "I hate to think what Mr. Maxwell will say when I tell him about all this!"

Frank spoke up. He could contain himself no longer. "Isn't Mr. Maxwell back from his trip?"

"No, he's not!" Peevey replied.

Frank, Joe, and Chet stared at one another, puzzled. They were each thinking the same thing. If Maxwell was still out of town, then who was the cigar-smoking prowler who'd been in Chet's room?

Peevey continued. "I have a phone number where Mr. Maxwell can be reached, and I'm going to call him just as soon as the police file their report."

Frank whispered to his brother. "That's strange! Yesterday he implied he had no idea where Mr. Maxwell was."

"You're right," Joe mumbled back. "I remember he said Maxwell was away somewhere, shopping for antiques."

"Something's fishy here," said Frank.

With the police upstairs, the guests had gone back to solving the mystery.

"Brad, you still haven't explained how your gum wrapper got into Iola's room," Matt said.

Brad pressed his forefinger into Matt's chest. "You think you're so hot! Well, I've got something on you, too, hotshot!"

He reached into his inside jacket pocket and pulled out Matt's paperback novel. "I found this on the grass under Iola's window!"

Matt gasped in astonishment. "How did that get there?"

"I'll bet it fell out of your pocket when you were making your getaway—*after* you stole Iola's necklace." Brad grinned triumphantly.

"That's not true!" Matt shouted. "Someone stole that book from me. I left it here in the parlor yesterday. When I came back for it, it was gone. For all I know, you took it just to try to shift the blame onto me!"

Brad laughed at him. "Yeah? Well, it's your word against mine!"

Frank and Joe moved between the two, trying to avoid physical confrontation. "Cool it, guys," Frank said calmly. "We've got enough problems without you two getting into a fight."

Brad moved away from Matt. "Anyway, I'm keeping the book as evidence."

"Give me my book back!" shouted Matt.

Joe took Matt aside and put an arm around his shoulder. "Matt, everyone's playing detective here this weekend, remember? That's what it's all about. You'll get your book back just as soon as the mystery is solved."

Matt muttered under his breath, "Some fun!"

The sound of footsteps was heard thundering on the stairs. A moment later the detective and two police officers entered the parlor.

"Okay, who's in room 207?" Detective Culp asked.

"That's our room, officer," the Hardys answered.

"Follow me," Culp ordered. Then he turned on his heel and left the room. Frank and Joe looked at each other quizzically and followed the shock of red hair up the stairs. The other two officers followed them.

The door to the Hardys' room was wide open, and a uniformed officer was standing guard outside. Culp gave the boys a verbal nudge. "Inside," he commanded.

Frank and Joe couldn't help wondering what was going on. And what was so important about their room? Perhaps the detective wanted to speak with them in private.

"Close the door, Sam!" Detective Culp said to one of the uniformed officers. Then he walked over to one of the beds and lifted the spread. "Look under here and tell me what you think this is!"

Frank and Joe knelt and peered beneath the bed. They both gasped. Spilling out of a canvas bag were all kinds of tools!

"I'll save you the trouble, and tell you what they are," said the detective. "Burglar's tools!"

"Burglar's tools!" both Hardys chorused.

"That's right," Culp's voice thundered. "You're under arrest!"

100

11 Tools to Build a Frame

"Under arrest, for what?" Joe blurted out.

"On suspicion of robbery!" growled Detective Culp. "It looks like you two might be responsible for our recent rash of hotel thefts."

Instantly, two of the uniformed officers grabbed them and pulled their arms behind their backs. The Hardys felt the cold steel of handcuffs being clamped on their wrists.

"Do you know who we are? We're—" Frank began, but was cut off by Detective Culp.

"I don't care who you are," he bellowed. "Those tools are safecracking tools."

"Somebody planted them there!" Joe cried in defense. "We're not thieves. I'm Joe Hardy and this is my brother, Frank. We're Fenton Hardy's sons!"

The detective chuckled. "Sure, and I'm Santa Claus! Come on. Let's go!" He moved them toward the door.

Frank mumbled, "Calm down, Joe." Then he spoke aloud in an even tone. "Officer, just let us explain—"

"Hold it!" Detective Culp put up his hand. "Before you say anything, I have to read you your rights." He produced a small card and began reading from it. "'You have the right—'"

Frank stopped him. "We know our rights, officer, and we're more than willing to tell you everything we know."

"Then tell it to the captain down at the station!"

The detective touched both Hardys on their shoulders to move them along the hall. "Sam, bring those tools and seal that door. No one's allowed inside until I say so!"

Obediently, the officer removed the canvas bag containing the tools. One of the other officers began unrolling yellow tape imprinted with the words: CRIME AREA—NO TRESPASSING. ORDER POLICE DEPARTMENT.

Frank and Joe's hearts sank as Detective Culp marched them down the stairs in handcuffs.

Peevey stood at the bottom of the stairs, his eyes widening as they passed him. "It just goes to show, you can't trust anyone these days!"

"We're innocent, Mr. Peevey," said Joe.

"Certainly doesn't look that way." Peevey looked down his nose at them. "I'm sure Mr. Maxwell will be shocked to learn that two of his guests have turned out to be the hotel thieves!"

"But we're not—" Joe started to say.

Frank stopped him by saying, "Forget it. He's not going to believe you."

Chet and Iola rushed out of the parlor and followed the Hardys down the front stairs and out to the driveway. They were clearly in shock.

"Don't worry about us," Joe told them before climbing into a patrol car. "It's just a misunderstanding."

Chet rushed to the window of the cruiser. "Is there anything we can do?"

Joe shrugged. "Just keep your eyes open!"

The patrol car's engine surged, and Chet and Iola stared in disbelief as the Hardys were taken away. When they turned around, they saw all of the guests lined up on the porch, watching the departure.

Finally Julie broke the tension. "Those police

officers were great!" she said cheerily. "They almost had me convinced they were real!"

Chet and Iola just looked at each other.

At the police station, Detective Culp questioned the Hardys at length about the reason for their visit to the Sky Blue Inn.

"You expect me to believe that you were hired by Mr. Maxwell to stage a mystery?" he asked.

The boys nodded.

"So where is Mr. Maxwell? I'd like him to verify your story."

"That's the problem," Frank said. "According to the manager, Mr. Peevey, Maxwell is out of town buying antiques for the inn."

"How inconvenient for you," said Culp. "So there's no one who can vouch for you."

"Yes, there is. Our father, Fenton Hardy," Joe said emphatically.

"You expect me to bother Fenton Hardy with a story like this?"

"But you've seen our identification," said Frank.

"Fake," retorted the detective.

Finally, the Hardys persuaded Detective Culp to make the call. In no time at all Fenton Hardy was telling him that the two boys were, indeed, his sons. He also confirmed that they had been hired to plot a mystery weekend for the Sky Blue Inn.

Frank was allowed to take the phone and spoke at some length with his father. He assured Mr. Hardy that they were all right, and detailed everything that had happened in the past two days.

"Looks like you boys have your hands full," Mr. Hardy said. "Do you need any help?"

"Thanks, Dad, but I think we can handle it," Frank said. "We're going back to the inn to do some work of our own."

"Okay, but if you run into any more problems, give me a call," said their father.

"Thanks, Dad. We'll keep you posted." Frank hung up the phone.

After some more questions, Detective Culp agreed to release the boys, provided they not leave the hotel without notifying him. "You're still suspects as far as I'm concerned."

Frank and Joe were shocked. "Even after talking with our father?"

A grim smile played on the detective's lips. "Sometimes the sons of law enforcement officers turn out to be bad apples."

As the Hardys left his office, he called after them. "From what I've heard, you two are supposed to be pretty good detectives. So if you turn

105

up anything—anything at all—call me immediately. I don't want you going off on your own trying to solve this case."

Frank and Joe were escorted out of the police station and into a patrol car. One thing was certain. In order to clear themselves completely, they had to catch the real thief—or thieves.

12 Trouble in the Air

"Why were you arrested?" Julie asked when the boys were back in the parlor at the inn.

"I heard they found a burglar's kit in your room," said Matt excitedly.

"If they caught you with the goods," asked Brad, "how come they released you?"

Even Iola joined in. "Were they real cops or phony?"

"Hold it, hold it!" Frank yelled over the barrage of questions. "One at a time, please!"

"We weren't exactly arrested. We were just taken in for questioning," Joe said.

"As suspects," added Brad in a suspicious tone. "They don't haul people down to the police

107

station unless they think they've got something on them."

Frank gave Brad a hard look. "As Joe said, they took us in for questioning. We were able to prove that we had nothing to do with the safe robbery."

"How were you able to do that?" Julie asked.

"I'm afraid that's confidential," said Joe.

"Oh, la-di-da!" exclaimed Julie. "Aren't you the mysterious ones! The next thing we know you'll be telling us you're CIA agents!"

"How'd you guess?" Joe grinned.

"What about those tools?" Iola asked. "How did you explain those?"

"Obviously, the tools were planted in our room to throw suspicion on us," explained Joe.

"Did the police buy that?" Matt asked. "All they have is your word on it."

"Let's just say it took a lot of convincing," Frank said.

"Look, we're going upstairs. It's been a rough day," Joe said.

The guests stood at the bottom of the stairs and watched the Hardys until they disappeared around the second-floor landing.

In their room Joe flopped down in an armchair while Frank sat on the edge of his bed. He looked seriously at Joe. "We're really in it now. We come up here to stage a mystery, and wind up being suspects in a real crime!"

Joe smiled in an effort to cheer his brother up. "All we have to do is catch the real thief and we'll be in the clear!"

Frank still looked troubled. "What gets me is that from the beginning, someone has been trying to scare us off. First that note on the brick. Then that creep on the black motorcycle."

"What about the spider—and the chemical in your food?" Joe added.

"Don't forget the bump on your head."

"How could I!" Joe said. "But what does it all mean?"

Frank stood and began pacing the floor. "It means that from the beginning, someone has known who we really are, and doesn't want us up here."

Joe exhaled deeply. "The only one who knows is Maxwell, and he hasn't even shown up yet."

"That *really* bothers me," Frank said. "Why did Maxwell decide to take off to buy antiques after he'd arranged for this weekend?"

Joe frowned. "Beats me. Unless he figured we were capable of handling it by ourselves. He went to great lengths to check us out, remember?"

"Yeah, but even the way he checked us out was weird . . . I mean, what did the whole mall thing prove?" Frank mused out loud.

"Did you notice anything funny about our room when the police were showing us the burglar's tools?" Joe asked.

"I'd forgotten to mention that," Frank said. "But so much has happened. There was the faint odor of cigar smoke lingering in the room, just like in Chet's."

"It wasn't just any old cigar, either."

"It was one of Maxwell's cigars," Frank said. "If Maxwell had been in our room earlier, he could have planted the burglar's tools under our bed!"

"*If* it was Maxwell," added Joe. "It's possible that someone else smokes Maxwell's brand."

"Possible, but not likely," Frank said. "It's too coincidental."

"Anyway, whoever it was went into Chet's room first. But why?"

Frank paced the floor some more. "The only reason I can think of is that he thought Chet's room was ours, realized his mistake, and then went into our room."

Joe shook his head. "You know it can't be Maxwell. Why would he try to frame us?"

"It doesn't make sense, does it?" Frank remarked.

There was a knock at the door. Joe gave Frank a quizzical look and crossed to open it.

Iola stood in the doorway holding a folded sheet of paper in her hand. "I found this slipped under my door!" She handed the note to Frank, who quickly opened it. He read it aloud.

"'Tell your friends to back off—or else!'"

"Another threat!" Frank muttered.

"Wonder what the 'or else' means," Iola said.

"Whatever you want it to mean, I guess," said Frank, frowning.

Iola gasped. "Aren't you afraid?"

"We'd be fools if we weren't," said Frank.

"Then why don't we just pack up and go home, right now?" suggested Iola.

"Not on your life!" cried Joe. "This kind of thing makes me want to push even harder!"

"Me, too," Frank said. "It makes me mad!"

Iola sighed. She knew the Hardys were too brave to be put off by scare tactics. "Please be careful," she said.

Frank studied her and then said, "You're in this, too, Iola. *All* of us have to be careful!"

Joe put a finger to his lips, warning both of

them to be quiet. "Shh!" He pointed to the door.

He tiptoed across the room. Then, with one swift movement, he jerked the door open.

Matt Spyle fell into the room.

"Matt! Fancy meeting you here!" exclaimed Joe.

"What were you doing listening at our door?" Frank asked angrily.

Matt stammered. "I wasn't listening. I—I dropped something in the hall, and I was looking for it."

"I see. And it just happened to drop near our door." Joe grimaced.

Matt squared his shoulders and stood up straight. "All right, what if I was listening! We're all playing detective this weekend, and I have a right to snoop!"

Frank pretended to be hurt. "Why us, Matt? Why not Julie or Brad or that Chet?"

Matt's face reddened. "I guess it's because you two are prime suspects."

"So you thought you might overhear something you could report to the police?" Joe asked.

Matt appeared sheepish. He looked down at the floor. "Something like that. I wasn't going to turn you in. For all I know this is just a fake crime, anyway!"

"Matt, we don't want to spoil your fun, and we

appreciate your trying to help," Frank said sincerely.

"Help?" Matt asked.

"Yes," Frank said. "Isn't that what you're doing? Helping us clear ourselves? You know we're innocent, don't you?"

"I—I guess so."

"In spite of the tools they found in our room?" offered Joe, going along with Frank.

Matt began nodding in agreement. "Yes, they could have been planted there."

"And in spite of the fact that you saw us outside Julie's room after she was robbed last night?" Frank asked.

"Yes," Matt said, remembering. "You chased me! You thought I'd burgled her room."

"How do you know that isn't what we wanted you to believe?" Joe asked with a mysterious tone in his voice.

Matt stammered. "I—I just assumed—well, what's your point? I'm totally confused."

"The point is, people can twist anything around to make anyone look guilty," explained Frank.

"We've got a proposition for you, Matt," Joe said, taking Frank's cue. "We need your help."

Matt's eyes brightened with excitement. "Anything you say. How?"

"Keep your eyes open," suggested Frank. "You work on the theft of Iola's necklace, and we'll work on the safe robbery."

Joe added, "Later, we'll compare notes and see if there's a connection."

"I see what you're getting at," Matt said with a knowing nod. "Good idea! I'll bet there is a connection!"

"Have we got a deal?" Frank asked.

"Deal!" Matt shook their hands and left, grinning.

The phone in their room rang, causing them all to jump. Joe grinned. "Looks like we're on edge, too!" He lifted the receiver.

"This is Mr. Peevey," the voice said over the phone. "Mr. Maxwell is down in the lobby and would like to see you both right away!" The phone was hung up with a loud click.

"Maxwell's here!" Joe announced. "He's waiting for us downstairs!"

Frank breathed a sigh of relief. "Finally, we'll get some answers!"

They took the stairs two at a time and sprinted across the lobby and into the office.

There, sitting behind Peevey's desk was—a complete stranger!

13 The Real Mr. Maxwell

"You're Mr. Maxwell?" Frank asked in astonishment.

"Of course," replied the tall, thin man angrily. "And who, might I ask, are you?"

Frank and Joe were speechless. Finally, Frank found his voice. "If you're the *real* Mr. Maxwell, then who was the man who met us at the Bayport Mall and hired us?"

"Bayport Mall?" asked the real Mr. Maxwell. "I don't know what you're talking about. Hired you? For what?"

"I think we'd better explain," Frank said.

"Yes, I think you'd better! Because you boys are in a lot of trouble!"

Frank and Joe related the events that led up to

their being hired by the man claiming to be Maxwell.

Maxwell grunted. "I know nothing about a mystery weekend. I've been away. I'd still be away, but I wasn't having any luck buying antiques, so I came back early."

"There was an ad in the newspaper," Joe said. "Your guests are here to take part in a mystery weekend!"

Maxwell looked at Peevey and said, "Do you know anything about this ad?"

Peevey showed his yellow teeth and simpered. "I never read the local papers, sir. I think this is just something these two boys have cooked up."

Frank and Joe were stung by the accusation.

"We'll be happy to call the newspaper and verify that an ad was placed by the Sky Blue Inn about a mystery weekend," Joe said.

"It's after five. The business office is closed," Peevey said, with a sneering smile.

"We'll call them first thing in the morning," Joe countered. "You'll see we're telling the truth!"

"Even if the ad *was* in the paper," said Maxwell, "what makes you think I'd believe you were hired to come here?"

"Our father is Fenton Hardy," Frank said. "Have you heard of him?"

"Of course. Everyone's heard of Fenton Hardy. I know all about him. But I've already spoken to Detective Culp, and he's told me that you're *still* under suspicion for robbery, even with your father's vouching for you."

"We have other witnesses who can confirm our story," Frank said. "They're guests right here at the inn. Chet and Iola Morton!"

Peevey eyed the two Hardys suspiciously. "When you checked in, you said Iola was your sister! Not this Morton's wife!"

"Not wife, his sister. That was part of our plan," Joe explained. "Iola pretended to be our sister so Chet could be a stranger. The theft of Iola's necklace was planned by us. Then we went around planting false clues. We tried to make it seem like all the guests might be guilty."

"The idea was for the guests to solve the mystery before the weekend was over," said Frank.

"Tomorrow we're supposed to expose Chet as the thief! And then we'll see who worked it out."

"That's the truth," said a voice. They turned to see Chet and Iola standing in the doorway. "It's what Mr. Maxwell hired us to do."

Frank gestured in the direction of the tall man. "Chet, this is the real Mr. Maxwell. The one who hired us was an impostor."

Maxwell shook his head. "This is all very confusing. I really should throw you all off my property. But, somehow, I find it difficult to believe that you could make up a story like this."

"You believe us?" asked Frank hopefully.

"I didn't say that," replied Mr. Maxwell, wiping his brow. "If someone is going around posing as me, I'd like to find out who it is. You boys are supposed to be detectives, right?"

Frank and Joe nodded and waited for him to get to the point.

"Since you're suspects, you'll want to clear yourselves. And I certainly want to get to the bottom of this."

"Our sentiments exactly," said Joe.

"Then, I'm going to give you twenty-four hours to come up with something," Mr. Maxwell said, continuing, "or else I'll be forced to press charges against you."

The Hardys were astounded. "Press charges?" asked Frank. "What for?"

"For committing a fraud against the Sky Blue Inn and its guests."

Frank and Joe felt anger rising in their chests. First they had been blamed for the safe robbery, and now for fraud!

"Believe me," promised Frank. "We're going

118

to do all we can to get the people responsible for this!''

Chet reached into his pocket and produced a torn clipping. ''For starters, here's a copy of the ad that appeared in the paper,'' he said, offering it to Maxwell.

Maxwell snatched it eagerly and read the ad. ''Amazing! Whoever placed this must have known I was going out of town!'' Then he looked at the Hardys and a grim expression crossed his face. ''But how do I know you didn't place the ad?'' he asked.

Joe exhaled deeply. ''You don't. But we're going to find out who did!''

Maxwell frowned. ''I don't mean to be hard on you, but all the evidence does point to you.''

''We understand,'' Frank said. ''We can't blame you.''

Maxwell stood up, indicating that their meeting was over. ''Now, I suggest we all have dinner and then try to get a good night's sleep!''

The next day the two Hardys took an early-morning walk around the grounds of the Sky Blue Inn so they could discuss the case in private.

''For all we know our room could be bugged,'' suggested Frank. ''That's why I asked you not to say anything about all this in our room last night."

"Well, there aren't any hidden microphones out here," Joe said, looking around just to make sure. "So what do you think?"

Frank bit his lower lip. "First of all, I think Peevey lied about the ad in the newspaper. He had to know about it. Everyone's been talking about the mystery weekend in front of him, and he's been going along with it."

Joe agreed. "He knows a lot more than he's telling, that's for sure! Do you think he's in on the safe robbery?"

"I'd be willing to bet on it," Frank said firmly. "Only we don't have a shred of proof."

"I've been suspicious of him ever since we found that silver dollar in our room after the spider incident."

"I've got him pegged as the one who planted that, too. The question is why?" pondered Frank. "What's the motive? Peevey's a perfect stranger to us. Why would he hassle us and lie to Mr. Maxwell just to get us in trouble?"

"Beats me," Joe said. "Unless he's working for someone else."

"Good point," Frank said grimly. "But who?"

The two continued walking down the grassy

120

knoll that surrounded the house until they spotted a large stone and wood building nearby. "Wonder what that is," Joe said.

"From the size of the doors, it must be a stable," Frank guessed.

"Come to think of it, Peevey mentioned they had a stable here," said Joe. "But he said it wasn't used anymore."

They headed toward the building. "Looks like the windows have been boarded up for years," Joe observed as they rounded the corner of the ancient stable.

Frank grabbed Joe's arm and held him back. "Wait a minute," he whispered, then pointed. "One of the barn doors is slightly open."

"Someone must be inside," said Joe.

They inched quietly around the rear of the building, hoping for another way in. Suddenly they heard the sound of hushed voices. Then, a tinkling sound.

"Hear that?" Frank whispered.

Joe nodded. "It sounded like somebody dropped something made of metal."

Frank gestured for Joe to stop, and the boys huddled beneath a window. The voices were louder, but they still couldn't make out what was being said.

Noticing one of the boards covering the window was loose, Joe stood up and pulled it out slightly so he could peer inside.

There, standing in the dusty sunlight that filtered in through the door, was the man who had pretended to be Mr. Maxwell!

He was speaking with someone who was hidden in shadow. Suddenly the heavyset man's eyes widened. He turned and ran!

"He spotted us!" cried Joe. "After him! He's going out the door. Quick! Before he gets away!"

The boys ran as fast as they could around to the front. Once there, they just caught sight of "Maxwell" as he topped the grassy knoll and headed toward the parking lot.

"Hurry, Joe!" Frank yelled. "That big guy's faster than he looks!"

The two Hardys ran up the hill, but the heavyset man already had a big lead on them. He leapt into his car, banged the door shut, and gunned the engine to life. And his companion had vanished!

Frank and Joe reached the lot just as the black car backed out of its space. Roaring straight ahead, the car suddenly swerved to the right and spun around. It was headed directly for the Hardys. With each second its speed increased.

"Look out!" yelled Joe. He and Frank dove,

one on either side of the car. The last thing they saw was the shiny chrome of the front grille, inches from their heads! They rolled along the pavement for a few feet before leaping up and heading for their own van.

"We can still catch him!" shouted Frank.

They scrambled in and switched on the ignition. Before the engine had turned over completely, they were in gear, the tires spinning. They burned rubber as the van sped out of the parking lot. Racing past the front entrance of the inn, they plunged down the winding road that led to the main gate. The black car was out of sight, just around a curve, but they could hear it picking up speed.

Just as they were about to reach the gate, a police cruiser pulled in from the main road and slid across the drive, blocking their way.

"Hold on!" Frank shouted. "We're going to crash!"

Instinctively, Joe reached out to help Frank pull hard on the wheel, forcing the van to the right. At the same time Frank stomped on the brake. Screaming, the tires tore into the gravel, throwing it out in a plume. The rear end fishtailed violently. The van came to a full stop, its nose crushing a small white pine, its rear up against the cruiser.

A uniformed officer slowly got out of the patrol car and sauntered toward the Hardys. They sat helplessly in their van, listening to the engine tick down. Two feet from the van, the officer drew his gun and shoved it forward through the open window. Frank jerked his head back, and heard the click of the hammer!

14 Secrets in the Stable

Frank and Joe just stared at the police officer, and the officer backed off and returned his gun to its holster.

"Weren't you told not to leave the grounds of the inn until this investigation was completed?" he bellowed.

"Yes, officer," Frank apologized. "But we were following a man who might have been able to provide evidence to solve this case."

"Sorry." The officer shook his head. "You aren't allowed to leave the grounds. Drive this van back up the hill! But first, I'll get the cruiser out of the way, if you don't mind."

Frank heaved a sigh while he waited for the

patrol car to move. Then he put the van in reverse and began backing away from the crushed white pine.

Joe sat angrily shaking his head from side to side. "I can't believe it! Just when we were getting close! Why do you think the cop didn't stop the black car?"

"He only had orders to stop the guests. Don't worry, we'll get another chance at our mystery man," said Frank. "I have a hunch we interrupted an important meeting. He'll be back."

"I wonder who the other guy was," said Joe.

"Remember the sound we heard just before we got to the window?" Frank said.

"Yeah. A tinkling sound."

"Like a coin rolling around, maybe?" Frank raised an eyebrow.

Joe nodded. "So you think this Mr. Whoever was talking with Peevey."

"It figures!" Frank said. "Peevey's always fiddling around with a silver dollar. If he's not spinning it on the counter, he's flipping it in the air!"

"He could've dropped it while talking with the Maxwell impostor. And when we chased them, he probably just went back into the inn."

Frank shifted the van into first and headed up

the winding driveway. "Let's go have a talk with our Mr. Peevey!"

The boys entered the lobby of the inn and stormed into the office. Peevey was nowhere to be seen. He wasn't in the parlor, either.

They looked down the long hall and saw Chet coming toward them. "There you are," he called out. "I've been looking all over for you. What's happening?"

"Have you seen Peevey?" Joe asked.

"Sure," Chet said. "He's in the kitchen seeing what's for lunch. I was just in there myself for the same reason."

The Hardys rushed past Chet. "Hey, wait for me!" he yelled, following them down the hall to the kitchen.

Peevey was standing in the doorway of the pantry with a clipboard in one hand. "Don't bother me now, boys. I'm busy taking inventory," he snapped, waving them off with a hand over his shoulder. "I haven't got time to play detective with you!"

"I'll bet you don't!" Frank said sharply. "But I think you'd better take the time, or else we'll do our talking with the police!"

Peevey asked the cook to step out of the room

for a minute. Then he smiled. His lips pulled back mechanically. "What can I do for you, boys?"

"We were just down by the stable and saw the man who posed as Maxwell!" Joe blurted out.

Peevey acted surprised. "Oh, really?"

"Yes," Frank said, moving in close to him. "He was talking with someone."

"And we think that someone was you," Joe said.

"Me?" Peevey laughed. "Sorry, boys. I've been here in the kitchen for the past half hour!"

Frank lowered his voice and sounded slightly menacing. "Listen. Our mystery man was talking with someone in the stable. And that someone dropped a coin while they were talking. That much we know for sure."

Peevey's face was a blank. Finally, he said, "So what does that prove?"

Frank gave him a hard look. "You're sure you weren't in the stable a little while ago, Mr. Peevey?"

Peevey stood up. "I don't know what you're talking about. And as far as dropping a coin goes, well, anybody can drop a coin! You've got nothing on me!"

With that he started to walk out of the kitchen.

He stopped at the door to the hall and said, "And I'll thank you to get out of the kitchen! Guests aren't allowed in here!"

They left, passing the cook as they walked out the back door. "Where are we going?" Chet asked. "It's getting close to time for lunch!"

"Let's have a look around that stable," Frank said. "We haven't had a chance to go over it yet."

The barn door, through which the mysterious strangers had fled, was still open, and the aroma of cigar smoke hung in the air.

"Find something?" Frank asked Joe, who was bent over, examining the floor.

"There are the two sets of footprints," he replied. "Lucky for us the floor is covered with dust!" He traced his finger in the powdery substance. Then he stopped short.

"Don't move!" he ordered.

Frank and Chet froze.

"Look at this!" Joe pointed to a round smudge in the dust.

"Open the door wider so I can have more light," Joe asked.

Moving carefully to avoid raising any dust, Frank and Chet eased the large barn door open wider. The strong late-morning sun poured in across the stable floor. They returned and bent down beside Joe.

There, in the thick white dust, was the impression of what could have been a large coin. A silver dollar, maybe!

"Peevey must have been here," Frank said. "But, wait a minute, what could have made the tinkling sound?" He glanced around. Lying near the impression was an upside-down galvanized tin tub. "Bingo, the coin must have hit the tub and then bounced.

"Peevey and that impostor must be in this thing together. This is the first real lead we've had!"

"Yeah," Joe agreed. "But we still don't have any proof that they stole the contents of the safe."

Frank nodded his head. "I'm afraid all this tells us is that Peevey *knows* the man who hired us to come up here. He's probably into this thing deeply, so we've got to watch his every move from now on!"

"Let's get back to the inn," suggested Joe. "We've got lots to do!"

"Not to mention lunch," Chet said. "I can smell it from here."

"Even through the stink of that cigar?" Joe asked.

"I can smell food anytime, anyplace." Chet grinned as he followed them out of the stable.

They entered the dining room just as lunch was being served. Brad Wilcox greeted them.

"I didn't think they'd let two fugitives from justice eat in the main dining room," he said.

"We're not fugitives!" snapped Joe, his temper flaring.

"Now, now, aren't we sensitive?" chided Brad. "What's the matter? Can't take a little joke?"

"I don't think you're very funny," Joe said.

"I think I'm hilarious," Brad said. "And you're still under suspicion by everyone at this table. Right?"

Everyone at the table nodded in agreement, except Matt Spyle. Brad noticed and said, "What's the matter, Matt? You mean to tell me that you trust these two?"

"A detective does not reveal his thoughts until the time is right," Matt said calmly. "I'm conducting my own investigation. And I'm coming up with some very interesting conclusions, which I'll relate when I'm ready!"

"Mr. Holmes is touchy!" said Brad sarcastically.

Iola tried to change the subject. "Brad, you still haven't explained why your gum was in my room just after my necklace was stolen!"

Brad squared his shoulders. "I don't have to explain it. I don't know how it got there any more than you do! And that's all I have to say."

"Now who's the touchy one?" said Iola. She smirked and turned to her plate.

Her voice full of excitement, Julie said, "Anyway, we only have a couple of hours left to solve the mystery. Someone stole my watch and camera, Iola's necklace, and robbed the office safe! The question is, who is that someone?" She was still caught up in the game.

Frank looked at her seriously. "Julie, you honestly think all this is just part of the mystery weekend, don't you?"

"Of course!" she answered brightly.

Frank let out a sigh. "What do the rest of you think? Do you think it's all a put-on?"

Everyone agreed. Matt said, "After all, we paid to get involved in a mystery, and judging from all that's going on, I feel I'm getting my money's worth. I'm having a great time."

Frank smiled. "And we're the prime suspects."

Julie said, "You sure are. Those police were really convincing."

There was a grim smile on Joe's face. "They convinced *us*, didn't they, Frank?"

Frank managed to chuckle. "Oh, yeah!"

The rest of the meal was uneventful. Later, while the others sat around and discussed the case, the Hardys went back to their room.

"Shouldn't we keep an eye on Peevey?" Joe asked.

"I asked Chet to do that. I think we should take another look around our room. We know the burglar's kit was planted, so someone had to plant it. Let's look around once more to see if we missed anything."

Joe groaned.

"Come on, just one more time."

The two Hardys began a careful search of their room. Finally, in the bathroom, Joe spotted something. On the white tile floor, under the bath mat, was some ash. Could it be cigar ash?

"How could we have missed this?" Joe asked.

"The bath mat was covering it. It could have gotten kicked over."

"I suppose the police didn't see it because once they found those tools," Joe said, "they stopped searching." He walked back into the bedroom and plopped down on the bed. "So, what do we do now?"

"Let me see that note Iola found under her door," said Frank.

Joe sat up and dug into his pocket. He handed

the note over. In the meantime, Frank had begun going through his suitcase and brought out a sheet of paper.

"What's that?"

"These are the original instructions that the fake Maxwell gave to us back at the Bayport Mall."

"Why are you dragging that out?" Joe asked.

"I want to compare it with this note," Frank explained. He spread both sheets out flat on the table and began examining them carefully. "Hand me my magnifying glass, Joe."

Joe reached into the pocket flap of Frank's suitcase and came up with the glass. "Here you go, Sherlock."

"Don't laugh," Frank said. "These things really do come in handy." Frank pored over the two typewritten sheets.

After a few minutes he looked up. "I'm positive now. Both of these pages were typed on the same typewriter!"

"Are you serious?" Joe was astonished.

"See for yourself," said Frank, handing Joe the magnifying glass. Joe took it and began studying the two pages.

"Pay special attention to the capital letters," Frank said. "Notice anything funny about them?"

Joe peered at them for a few more moments. "I see it now! The capital letters on both typewritten sheets are raised slightly!"

"Indicating that there's something wrong with the shift mechanism on that particular typewriter."

Joe beamed. "Meaning that those instructions and that note were typed by the same person!"

"At least the same typewriter!" Frank said. "No question about it!"

There was a knock on the door. Frank opened it, and Chet entered.

"Hey, aren't you watching Peevey?" Joe asked.

"I lost him."

"What do you mean you lost him?" asked Joe. "How could you?"

"I went out to the kitchen for just a minute to see if there was a little snack I could have to hold me to dinner, and when I went back he was gone," Chet said quietly. "What's happening with you?"

They explained to him about the typewritten notes. Chet rubbed his chin and said, "It looks like this case is finally shaping up."

Frank continued, "And I'll bet that typewriter is somewhere in this inn!"

Chet sat down on the edge of Joe's bed. He appeared to be deep in thought. After a minute he said, "I'm just trying to remember about when I checked in. There was luggage still in the lobby, and I'm sure there was a portable typewriter next to it. The guy came along and carried it upstairs himself. It was—"

Suddenly there was a loud crack, and the bedside lamp shattered, sending shards of glass flying.

15 The Whole Truth

The Hardys and Chet dove to the floor as the sound of the shot echoed in the room. They lay flat on the carpet, waiting for a second shot to ring out.

"Somebody's out to get us—and they mean business," Frank whispered.

"What are we going to do?" Joe asked. "We can't lie here forever."

"That b-bullet barely missed me!" stammered Chet. "If I lift my head, they might try again!"

"Stay still," Frank warned his friend. "I've got an idea!" He signaled Joe to follow him.

Moving slowly, the two brothers slithered on their bellies toward the window. When they reached it, they slid their bodies up against the wall on either side of it. They loosened the sashes and the drapes fell across the window.

They each breathed a loud sigh of relief. "You can get up now, Chet," Frank said. "Just don't stand directly in front of the window in case our marksman friend decides to fire blindly through the drapes!"

Chet stood up and shook his head. "The next time you guys offer to take me on a fun weekend, remind me that I have to stay home and work in the yard," he said.

Frank didn't answer. He was at the window, daring a quick peek outside.

"Be careful!" Joe said. "Whoever's out there is a good shot."

Frank slowly moved an edge of the drape aside and peered out. "There's a tall tree close by. Our sniper must have taken his shot from behind it. At any rate, he's gone now."

"Are you sure?" asked Chet, still doubtful.

"It's the only place he could have hidden," Frank replied. "We're safe."

"For now," Joe said meaningfully.

Frank turned to Chet. "You were about to tell us who checked into the inn with a portable typewriter."

"Oh, yeah," said Chet, still a little shaken from the experience. "It was Brad Wilcox. While

Peevey was getting my room key, Brad came along and picked up the typewriter. He made some snide remark to Peevey that he was tired of waiting for Botts to take it upstairs so he'd do it himself."

"So Brad has a typewriter," said Frank.

"Yeah, an old portable. The case was really battered," Chet remembered.

"That could explain why the caps are faulty," said Joe.

Frank sat on the edge of his bed and rubbed his palms on the knees of his pants. "We've really got our work cut out for us."

"Got a plan?" Chet asked. "Now that we know Brad typed both the instructions and the threatening note to Iola?"

Frank shook his head. "But we don't know that. All we really know is that Brad checked in with a typewriter. We still have to *prove* that it's the typewriter that was used to write those letters."

Joe scoffed. "We can't exactly go up to Brad and ask him, can we?"

"No," replied Frank. "But if we can get to Brad's typewriter without him seeing us, we could type a sample for comparison."

"I guess we could sneak into his room," Joe suggested.

"What if he walks in on us?" Frank asked.

Both Hardys turned and looked at Chet.

Chet became instantly wary. "Why are you staring at me?"

"Got a challenge for you, Chet," said Frank.

Chet threw up his hands. "Look, guys, I've been through enough for one day. For one lifetime! I just got shot at, remember?"

"There'll be no risk involved," Frank assured him.

"Sure, I thought there was no risk involved in coming into your room, either," muttered Chet. "And look what happened!"

Frank put both hands on Chet's shoulders. "There'll be a lot more risk if you don't help us, Chet."

"Frank's right," Joe said. "If we don't get to the bottom of this, we're *all* going to be sitting ducks!"

Chet shook his head. "I'm sorry, guys. I was just a little shook up for a moment. What would you like me to do?"

"Way to go," Frank said. "I knew we could count on you! It's simple. Go downstairs, find Brad, and talk to him. Keep him occupied."

Joe added, "Get into an argument with him if you have to! Anything to keep him downstairs long enough for us to check out his typewriter."

"Sounds simple enough." Chet grinned. "I'm good at irritating people."

All three laughed. "We'll follow you down to make sure you've cornered Brad. Then we'll slip back upstairs and do our snooping."

They found Brad sitting in the parlor watching television. Frank and Joe stayed in the hall while Chet struck up a conversation with him.

"What's up, Brad?" they heard Chet say to him. "I thought you'd be playing detective with the rest of the group."

"I don't have to play detective," Brad snarled. "I know who's guilty. I'm just hanging around to watch it all unfold."

In the hall Frank nudged Joe. "Chet's got him hooked. Let's go!"

Quietly, the Hardys turned and made their way back upstairs. When they reached the second floor, they saw a maid enter Brad's room. "Quick!" Frank said softly. "Get me a piece of tape. In my suitcase. With the magnifying glass."

Joe was gone and back in less than twenty seconds. Frank took the tape from him and peeked into Brad's room.

The maid, carrying towels, was just entering the bathroom.

Frank quickly placed the tape across the striker plate so the door wouldn't lock when the maid closed it. Then he and Joe returned to their room and waited.

Soon they heard the maid go into another room. The Hardys slipped across the hall and tried the door. It opened easily. Frank removed the tape, and they stepped inside.

"Good trick, Frank," Joe said.

"Thanks. Saw it in a movie once," Frank said.

Their eyes searched the room until they spotted the typewriter sitting on a small writing table.

They both moved toward it. Frank opened the battered case, removed a blank sheet of paper from his jacket, and inserted the paper into the machine.

"I'll type the exact message Iola found under her door," he said. " 'Tell your friends to back off—or else!' "

He removed the paper and compared it with the original. The type was exactly the same!

"Now we've got him!" Joe exclaimed. "Brad typed those directions *and* the threatening note!"

"No, all we know is that this typewriter was used," Frank said cautiously. "Brad has to have at least one partner. What about the phony Mr. Maxwell—and Peevey?"

Joe looked around the room. "As long as we're here, let's see what else we can find."

The thought made Frank uneasy. He said, "Okay. But we'd better hurry!"

They both headed in the same direction— toward the closet. "I see we both have the same idea." Frank grinned.

"You bet!" Joe said. "I'm dying to have a look at the soles of Brad's shoes!"

There were two pairs of shoes in Brad's closet: black dress loafers and sneakers. Frank picked up the sneakers and examined their soles. He held them up for Joe to see.

Joe nodded. "A waffle-grid pattern!"

"They look like they're the right size, too," said Frank.

Joe was puzzled. "Brad was behind this the whole time. But why?"

"Now we've got you!" a voice suddenly boomed out from behind them. Frank and Joe turned, startled.

Brad stood in the doorway. Behind him was Peevey—with a gun in his hand!

A snarl curled Brad's upper lip. "I've got you right where I want you," he said, gloating. "We caught you robbing my room!"

Peevey smiled and leveled the gun at the boys'

midsections. "This is too good to be true," he said.

"We're not taking anything from your room and you know it," Frank said angrily.

Brad laughed. "I know that! But the police won't! You're still under suspicion as far as they're concerned. And now you've been caught red-handed in my room. And Mr. Peevey is my witness!"

Peevey gave them a joyless smile. "We've got enough to put you both away for a long time!"

"You'll never get away with this," Joe said. "We've got evidence that proves you're the one who robbed Julie's room!"

"Oh, yeah?" Brad grinned. "It's your word against mine. And right now, I bet the police will believe me!"

Frank's voice was steady. "You framed us, Brad. We know it, and you know it!"

Brad couldn't help boasting. "Sure, I framed you. And for a couple of so-called smart guys, you sure fell for it."

"But why, Brad?" Frank asked. "Why are you out to get us?"

"Ever hear the name Joe Wingo?" Brad threw the question out like a whip.

"Joe Wingo!" Both Hardys uttered the name at the same moment. Then Frank said, "He was the head of a gang of criminals who operated on the East Coast. Our father—"

Brad interrupted. "That's right! Your father sent my father to prison!"

"Joe Wingo is your father?" Joe said, astonished.

"Right again," said Brad darkly.

"So you came after us," said Frank.

"Exactly," Brad continued. "I took my time, though. Waited until things cooled down. I planned this whole thing very carefully. I wanted to get you good! At first I thought of just coming after you with a gun, but then, I figured I'd probably get caught and wind up in prison myself. Then it came to me! Why not set up the Hardy boys so *they* wind up in prison?"

"That's your idea of justice?" said Frank.

"Poetic justice," said Brad. "The thought of you two in prison, the reputation of the Hardys ruined forever—you can't even imagine how happy that made me!" Brad smiled with evil satisfaction.

"Who was the man at the Bayport Mall who posed as Mr. Maxwell?" Frank asked.

"Lou," Brad answered, still smiling. "A friend of the family. He was in prison with my dad and got paroled. While he was inside, he promised my dad that he'd help me get the Hardys!"

Joe interrupted. "So when Lou got out of the joint, the two of you cooked this up?"

"Right." Brad smirked. He nodded toward the desk clerk. "Peevey used to work for my father. He's a master safecracker. When we found out he was working at the Sky Blue Inn, we decided it was a perfect setup. We'd pull a few jobs around here and then get you blamed for them."

"You're responsible for the hotel robberies in this area?" Joe said.

"All part of the plan," Brad bragged. "We figured as long as we were framing you, we might as well make a few bucks. There isn't a safe Peevey can't open. So we hit a few hotels, then set you up to take the fall!"

"Why the mystery weekend?" Joe asked.

"We figured it would be the perfect way to bait you into coming up here. It was Peevey's idea."

"And we walked into it, with our eyes wide open," Frank said bitterly.

"Walked?" Brad guffawed. "You *jumped* into it!"

"Who hit me on the head?" asked Joe.

"Lou, but that wasn't planned. You walked in on him," Brad said.

"Who fired the shot through the window?" Joe asked.

Peevey cleared his throat. "I did that. I only

meant to scare you. I may be a lot of things, but I'm not a killer." He looked down at the gun in his hand and added, "That is, unless I'm forced into it."

Suddenly Chet appeared in the doorway behind Brad and Peevey. "Sorry, guys. I kept him busy as long as I could—"

Peevey turned for an instant. An instant was all Frank needed. He let fly with a karate kick that sent Peevey's gun clattering to the floor.

Before Frank could regain his balance, Brad leapt on top of him, and they both fell wrestling to the floor.

Chet grabbed Peevey from behind and held him in a tight armlock. "Hold it. You're not going anywhere!"

Joe turned to watch Frank and Brad battling it out on the floor. Chet shouted, "Aren't you going to help Frank?" He was still struggling with Peevey.

Joe grinned. "What? And spoil Frank's fun? He hasn't had this good a workout in a long time!"

Joe leaned against the doorway with his arms folded and watched his brother expertly flip Brad over and pin him to the floor.

Frank held Brad flat to the floor, his fist poised in the air, ready to strike if necessary. "You were

147

the one who followed us on the motorcycle, too, weren't you?"

Brad nodded.

"You slashed our tire, tampered with my food, and made it look as though someone was trying to stop us from coming here! If you wanted us here, why did you try to scare us off?"

Brad smirked. "You think you're so smart! Well, I'm smarter than both of you. I did those things to bait you. I knew the more I tried to scare you away, the more intrigued you'd be. You fellows like a challenge, so I gave you one."

Frank shot a glance at Joe. "He had us pegged, all right."

A voice boomed behind them.

"I've heard enough!"

16 "Who Done It?"

Irwin Botts, the handyman, stood in the doorway with a gun in his hand. Behind him was the real Mr. Maxwell.

"We heard everything," said Botts. Then he ordered, "Peevey, Brad, I want both hands against the wall!"

After Chet and Frank let go of their assailants, the two criminals did as they were told. Botts smiled and turned to Frank and Joe. "It's called assuming the position. From what I've just heard, these two fellows must know it very well."

"Then you know we were framed," said Joe.

Maxwell smiled and shook Joe's hand. "I must admit, I didn't trust you two for a while, but after

149

talking with Botts, I realized it would be a good idea to let you conduct your own investigation. It seems you do have quite a reputation as detectives."

"A reputation we came close to losing," Frank admitted.

Maxwell grasped Frank's hand in a firm grip. "I don't know what to say, except 'thank you!' That hardly seems enough for what you've accomplished. Thanks to you, all the hotel robberies have been solved!"

"We're very glad things worked out the way they did," said Frank.

Botts interrupted. "Mr. Maxwell, call the police and tell them Detective Botts has a couple of presents for them."

"Detective Botts?" Frank and Joe asked at the same time.

Botts flipped open his wallet to show his badge. "I've been working undercover here as a handyman ever since these robberies began. I knew Peevey had a record; that's why I signed on here. I wanted to keep an eye on him. We weren't sure if Peevey was following the straight and narrow. Turns out, he wasn't."

"What about Brad's friend Lou?" asked Joe. "He's still at large."

Botts grinned. "The police will put out an APB on him. He won't get far. He doesn't know he's been fingered."

Later, as Botts and the police took Brad and Peevey off to the police station, Frank turned to Chet and Iola and saw the relief glowing in their faces. "We've had lots of close calls," Frank said, "but this is the first time we've come close to losing our reputation."

Later that day, everyone gathered in the lobby. The guests had lots of unanswered questions, so Frank and Joe suggested they all assemble in the parlor.

"This mystery weekend turned out to be more than we bargained for," Frank said. "The interesting thing is that part of the mystery was fake and part of it was real. Very real, indeed!"

"Exactly who planned all this, anyway?" Julie asked.

Joe smiled. "Frank and I planned the fake mystery. We were hired to set up a phony robbery and plant clues."

"I see," Julie said. "And the robbery of my room was part of that."

"No, I'm afraid the robbery of your room was real," Joe explained. "You'll get your valuables

151

back from the police as soon as the case is officially closed."

"I was really robbed!" Julie pressed her hand to her mouth and sat down in shock. When she had calmed down a little, she asked, "Who planned the real robberies?"

"Peevey," said Frank, going on to explain what had happened.

Joe completed the story. "So Brad was responsible for all the scare tactics to bait us."

Julie asked, "Who planted the burglar's tools in your room?"

"Lou. He'd been hiding in the stable, supervising the operation. Brad helped him."

"That explains the awful cigar smell in my room," said Chet.

"Sure," Joe said. "Lou went into your room by mistake. He intended to plant those tools in our room. When he realized his mistake, he left."

"When did you begin to suspect Brad?" Julie asked curiously.

Frank explained how Brad's typewriter provided the clue that did him in.

Julie nodded thoughtfully. "So you compared the two letters and put two and two together. Great work, guys!"

Just then Matt Spyle charged into the room in the company of a uniformed police officer. He pointed to Chet. "There he is, officer! Arrest him! He's the one who stole Iola's necklace!"

Before anyone could stop him, the officer had grabbed Chet and twisted his arm behind his back.

"Hey, what is this?" Chet asked as the police officer produced a pair of handcuffs.

"You thought you could get away with it, didn't you?" Matt grinned triumphantly. "But my clever deductions have proved to be your downfall!" He produced an empty candy box.

"I found this in Iola's room. Knowing your appetite and fondness for food, I realized that you were guilty. When you were stealing Iola's necklace, you couldn't resist eating all her chocolates! Iola told me she hadn't even opened the box. You're the only one here who could have done it."

Frank and Joe burst out laughing. "Congratulations, Matt! You've solved the mystery!"

Matt looked puzzled. "Wait a minute! You mean this one was a fake?"

Everyone laughed while Joe and Frank shook hands with him. "You did it, Matt. You stuck with it and came up with the right answer," Joe said.

Matt half smiled. "Yeah, the right answer to the wrong crime!"

Frank grinned. "Matt, that was the mystery you were supposed to solve. And you did it!"

Finally Matt beamed. "I guess you're right! I really did, didn't I? Maybe I am a pretty good detective after all!"